I0520110

THE
TRIBERS
BOOK OF DREAMS

K.N. VOGEL

ISBN 978-0-9875164-3-5

thetribers.com
https://www.facebook.com/THETRIBERS
https://twitter.com/TheTribers

Contents

Dedicated to the reader—

Create your own path,
Cherish the spirit within,
Celebrate life and always believe in infinite possibilities . . .

1

Midnight Meeting

There was a pause, and the dimly-lit room filled with applause. Sy Middleton clapped louder than anyone. He was so proud of his dad. Trent Middleton had made the bold move to leave investment banking and pursue his passion for independent filmmaking and environmental causes; and now here they were, celebrating the film he'd produced and directed. Sy loved how his dad had told the story and exposed the truth about pollution in the world's oceans.

The lights came up as the final credits disappeared. Sy's dad took a deep breath and stood up to thank the film crew and close friends who'd gathered at the Ryderson warehouse on Ninth Avenue in Manhattan's Meatpacking District for a private screening.

"Thank you to the film crew, my beautiful wife Rebecca, and son Sy. Your encouragement and belief in the cause inspires me every day. And finally, a special thanks to Samuel Ryderson." His dad gestured to an older, distinguished-looking man seated in the front row. His silver hair was cropped in a crew cut and he was dressed impeccably, a red handkerchief tucked into the lapel of his Brooks Brothers suit. "Your support has made my dream a reality."

Samuel stood and smiled. "Thank you, Trent. This is an exceptional achievement. You've produced a gift for future generations, and I'm proud to have been part of it."

Sy rose and accompanied his parents to the next room for refreshments. He was already tall, and his mom said he promised to be broad across the shoulders, like Trent. He brushed his dark-blond hair from his eyes. It was longish and cut in the latest style, framing his large brown eyes.

His dad was the center of attention, one arm firmly around his mom as he graciously accepted the praise from well-wishers. Sy took an extra-large handful of shrimp from a passing waiter, earning him a warning look from Rebecca.

Samuel and Trent embraced, congratulating each other. Sy knew they'd become close friends through the project. A teenager, slightly older than Sy, patted Trent on the back. He seemed super-confident, good-looking with spiked dark-brown hair; looking pretty cool in slim-cut black jeans and a striped shirt.

Samuel introduced him proudly. "My grandson, Joshua."

Joshua nodded to Sy. "Hey." His penetrating turquoise eyes seemed to sparkle with mischief.

"Hi," said Sy, shyly.

Samuel gestured to the rest of the warehouse apartment. "Why don't you show Sy around?"

The boys left the gathering and walked down a long corridor with artwork on the walls. Passing through the industrial-style kitchen, Sy looked in awe through huge windows that looked out on the Hudson River.

"I'll show you my room," said Joshua.

So, Sy thought, he lives with his grandfather—I wonder why? But he was distracted by his claustrophobic fear of small places, which rose up as Joshua led him to an elevator. "Are there stairs?" he asked.

Joshua raised his eyebrow. "There are five levels."

"I'm not good with elevators."

Joshua shrugged. "Sure thing," he said. "Call me Ryder—everybody does."

"How old are you?" asked Sy.

"Fifteen." Ryder narrowed his eyes, assessing Sy. "And you're thirteen, right?"

Sy nodded.

They climbed to the third floor.

"Second floor is Grandpa's library, third is his laboratory. He still works on experiments." Ryder pointed up. "I'm on the top floor."

They climbed the stairs to Ryder's "room"—a giant

space that seemed to cover the entire level. Sy's eyes nearly fell out of his head. There was a complete entertainment area with arcade games, pool table and air hockey. In another section was a gym set-up with free weights, bench press and a punching bag. Sy felt a stab of irritation toward his parents. He was currently arguing with them to put a measly computer and TV in his bedroom.

"Awesome!" was all he could manage.

They gravitated to the video games. Ryder seemed to have all the latest, and he seemed so easygoing and friendly.

"Where are your folks?" Sy asked.

Ryder didn't take his eyes off the giant TV. "My parents died when I was five." He was moving the animated characters with wild hand gestures, but Sy heard the pain in his voice, despite his glib attitude.

"I moved to Manhattan and my grandparents raised me. They were the only family I had. My grandma died a few years ago, and now it's just Grandpa Samuel and me."

No parents! Sy took a deep breath. How did Ryder handle it?

"Don't stress. I can't change it, so I've accepted it. And don't feel too sorry for me—I've had a great time with my grandparents. Grandpa's traveled and worked all over the world. He really is an incredible person. It's like he's lived a thousand lives," Ryder said with pride.

"What does he do?"

"He's an Ivy League professor, a leading world expert in quantum physics, an inventor, property developer and a bunch of other stuff."

Which explains the lab, thought Sy.

"He's also on the Board of a lot of charities and museums in Manhattan. He has really strong principles and backs causes that fight against any type of injustice. Like your dad's movie." Ryder stretched. "Want a game of pool?"

"Absolutely."

Sy was having a great time. He couldn't remember ever feeling so comfortable with someone he'd just met—or with people he'd known for ages, for that matter. Rebecca said he was "naturally introverted," and maybe that was true because it usually took him time to connect with people.

The elevator door opened, and Samuel, Trent and Rebecca joined them.

"Time to go," said his dad, gently. Sy could tell he was pleased to see that they had been getting along. "What a fabulous space," Trent exclaimed, looking around.

"Yeah, Dad," said Sy a little too loudly.

Samuel and his parents laughed, but Sy doubted he was any closer to getting a decent set-up for his bedroom.

"Let's walk our guests out, Joshua," said Samuel.

They exchanged goodbyes with promises of getting together soon. Ryder held out his hand and Sy shook it.

"Catch ya soon, Sy," he said.

* * *

"So what did you think?" Ryder asked his grandfather as they cleaned up in the kitchen.

"He has great potential."

"I really wanted to say something when we were playing pool." Ryder separated the beverage cartons for recycling. "I kind of felt like I should have."

"No, you must follow protocol," Samuel warned. "Make sure you look after Sy. He's going to need your support."

Ryder nodded. He knew better than to probe. Samuel always had a reason.

* * *

In the cab on the way home, Sy filled his parents in on every detail of Ryder's awesome room, even though they'd just seen it for themselves. "I'm the only one in my class who doesn't even have my own computer," he fumed. "You keep treating me like I'm a kid!"

Trent and Rebecca chose not to respond, and the cab headed uptown in silence. After a while, Rebecca suggested they invite Samuel and Joshua over for dinner. Sy didn't answer. He was still seething.

"Hey," she said. "Give your dad a break. After all, it's been a special night for him."

Sy relented. "Your film is awesome, Dad," he said.

The cab slowed to turn into Seventy-Ninth Street, in the Upper East Side, and stopped in front of their established brownstone. Sy noticed that the recently restored apartment building a few doors up had two big stone gargoyles fixed on either side of its entrance. "Freaky," he said.

Trent tipped the driver generously and they went inside. Everyone said his mom had a great sense of style. She'd decorated their townhouse, and it had been written up in *Town and Country* magazine. All Sy could be bothered with was a quick goodnight. He was exhausted, and from the look of them, his parents were too.

His bedroom looked a lot smaller than when he'd left it. Dropping his clothes to the floor, he changed into pajamas, yawned loudly and climbed into bed, glad it was Friday.

* * *

He woke. The townhouse was silent except for his dad, snoring softly. Had he just been dreaming? He was sure he'd just had a profound dream, but when he tried to recall the details, he drew a blank.

He turned over, hoping to find sleep again.

Someone nudged him gently. It can't be morning

yet, he thought, refusing to open his eyes. The nudging became more persistent. Annoyed, Sy sat up and switched on his reading lamp. He started in shock. Standing in his room, fully dressed and grinning, was Joshua Ryderson.

2

Dreamtime

"About time you woke up," said Ryder. He wasn't alone. Standing near the window were a stocky teenaged boy with sandy hair and lots of freckles, and a girl with long blonde hair and sky-blue eyes that slanted upward. She was gorgeous. Sy wanted to say something, but his mouth seemed glued shut.

"Meet Xanthia and Raf, friends of mine. We're here to help you become initiated as a triber," said Ryder, clearly enjoying himself.

Was this some sick joke? Was Ryder in a cult? Sy's voice returned and rose with each question. "Ryder, what are you doing in my house? How did you get in? Who are these people, and *what is a triber*?"

"Calm down, man," said Raf.

Sy wasn't going to allow some stranger to tell him how to behave. Outraged, he got out of bed quickly and lost his balance, suddenly dizzy.

"That's okay—it's perfectly normal. It'll take

some time for you to adjust," Xanthia reassured him, coming closer. She gestured to the bed. "Even though you're awake, there's a part of you that is still asleep."

Sy's body was still lying in the bed, fast asleep. What? How could this be? He was awake and asleep at the same time?

"It's called Dreamtime," said Ryder, answering his unasked question. "And is only possible for tribers."

Sy reckoned they had two minutes to explain or he was going to scream so loud that not only would Trent be in his room in a flash, but so would the neighbors. "What is a triber?" he asked, suspiciously.

"Tribers are select teenagers, chosen by the Zodiac Council to join one of four tribes: Earth, Fire, Air and Water," Ryder said, making himself comfortable by sitting on Sy's desk. "There's more to the universe than what most people know."

Xanthia sat on the end of his bed. It was so weird to see her sitting next to his sleeping body. "Once you're a triber, you get access to the Middle Realm," she said. "It's a hidden world, like a parallel universe that's invisible to everyone, except those who've been initiated into one of the four tribes—and for the mythical creatures who live there, of course."

Yeah, right, *of course*, thought Sy. "Parallel universe?" he said skeptically.

"It's another dimension, a place where magic happens all the time and anything is possible." Xanthia used her hands to demonstrate. "It kind of sits above the Lower Realm, in the sky."

Right. "So, who's the Zodiac Council?" Sy asked, playing along.

Raf spoke up from near the window, with great respect in his voice. "The Zodiac Council are the governing force in the universe. They protect and maintain Universal Law among all living beings across all realms." He looked sharply at Sy. "They choose the tribers," he said. "And you've been chosen. We're here to escort you out of the Lower Realm and into the Middle Realm. It's your turn to be initiated into Earth-tribe, just like us!"

Ryder jumped off the desk. "We need to go."

Sy didn't move.

"Give him a minute, Ryde," said Xanthia, touching his shoulder gently. "He needs some time."

Sy's mind was working overtime trying to absorb what he was being told. It was not even possible. How could it be possible? It was surreal. He hadn't even known Ryder a few hours ago! "Does Samuel know where you are?" he blurted. Maybe mentioning the grandfather he obviously adored would shame Ryder into telling the truth.

"Samuel? Sure," said Ryder, not missing a beat. "He's Triber-elite. Been an Earth-triber since he was a teenager."

Sy couldn't imagine Samuel as a teenager. Nor

could he believe that someone as respected as Samuel would be involved in such a hoax! Ryder was clearly deranged. The question was, was he dangerous?

Raf was looking around his room. Sy flushed as he remembered he was wearing pajamas. No sooner did he have that thought than the clothes he'd thrown on the floor appeared back on his body. He glanced uneasily at the part of himself that was still wearing pajamas, asleep in the bed. Perhaps this was all a dream.

Xanthia stood up. "Tribers can be awake and asleep and function as normal in both states," she said. "You access Dreamtime when you reach a certain level of sleep that varies for each individual. The body that you can see on the bed sleeps soundly—in a sort of meditative trance—and you both awake refreshed in the morning with full memory of all you did, even if you've been out all night." Her blue eyes shone with sincerity. "If you are woken abruptly, you will be teleported instantly back to your body."

Sy was silent.

"All new recruits take time to adjust to life as a triber," she finished gently. "Just because you don't understand it yet, doesn't mean it isn't true."

Sy allowed his mind to open up just a tiny bit.

Raf's palm glowed green. "We need to get going," he said.

Ryder nodded impatiently and started pacing.

"Ignore them," Xanthia told him. "You take your time."

But Sy still felt undecided.

Ryder stopped pacing. "Come on, Sy . . . join us," he pleaded. He looked so sincere.

Sy was quiet, irresistibly intrigued. Impulsively, he nodded and took a step toward the others.

"Sy, we're going to fly with you to basecamp," said Xanthia, clearly pleased with his decision.

Sy experienced a thrill of anticipation. Fly?

"Once you're initiated, you'll fly solo," said Ryder.

Xanthia held up both hands to Sy, and a beam of green light shot out and spread itself over him. He watched it permeate his body and was still mute as, seconds later, he felt himself lifted in the air. He was . . . flying! The group drifted to his closed window. Sy contracted in an involuntary cringe and shut his eyes but, amazingly, they just glided straight through. He didn't feel anything!

Sy found himself in the cool night air, hovering above his home. "How did we do that?" he asked in disbelief.

Xanthia laughed. "Part of Dreamtime is the ability to fly through solid objects, but only in the Lower Realm," she said.

Someone walked along the street below. "What if they see us?" Sy asked nervously.

"Don't worry," said Xanthia. "When you're in

Dreamtime, you're invisible to non-tribers." She held up her left palm. "Where is basecamp?" she asked. Another green beam shot from her palm, lighting the night sky.

"Straight to begin with," said Raf, leading the way. Xanthia and Ryder flew close to Sy. They ascended slowly above the Manhattan skyline. Sy felt free and weightless. Flying was totally insane.

"Sy, the Middle Realm will *blow your mind*!" said Ryder.

Sy caught Xanthia's amused look at Ryder's excitement, but he had to admit his enthusiasm was contagious. In spite of worrying that he might drop like a stone out of the sky at any minute, Sy was looking forward to what might happen next.

* * *

Ryder watched Sy closely, thrilled that he'd agreed to join them. Ryder had recently become a team leader, but Sy wasn't going to be in his team so he'd asked Xanthia and Raf if he could join them to lead their new recruit to initiation. It was a bit unorthodox, but Ryder was going to keep his promise to Samuel: he'd make sure he had Sy's back in the Middle Realm.

3

The Middle Realm

They continued upward, the lights of Manhattan disappearing below. Out of the darkness, a spinning mini-twister of colored light headed straight for them. Sy stiffened and looked to the others, but they were smiling indulgently. The light spun around Ryder like a firefly until it finally slowed down to reveal a small creature.

"Hey, Ryder," the creature said. He nodded at Raf, and with the deferential tone reserved for celebrities, said, "Xanthia."

Xanthia grinned as she matched his tone. "Levi."

Levi was about half Ryder's size, with large ears and round, dark-green eyes. He was wearing a well-tailored pinstripe suit with a black tee. On his little feet he wore the coolest new trainers.

Levi gestured to Sy. "Who's this?"

"Meet Sy. He's being initiated tonight," said Ryder.

"I'm Levi of the Polooza Pixies." He held out his hand to shake. "You have heard of me."

It wasn't a question. Sy remained quiet, not wanting to offend.

Levi seemed quite put out. "You haven't heard of me!"

"He hasn't even joined the Earth-tribe yet. Give him a chance," said Ryder.

"So, what's up?" asked Raf.

"I want to remind you about my party. It's happening after the next full moon, and it's going to be sick. You're still coming, aren't you? Bring your entourage." Levi pointed at Sy. "Him, too."

"We'll be there," promised Ryder.

"Including you?" Levi asked Xanthia, pointedly.

"Sure," she promised.

"Okay, gotta blaze," said Levi, and promptly disappeared.

"Was he a real pixie?" asked Sy.

Ryder grinned. "Yep. Pixies, elves, trolls, gnomes and many other creatures live in the Middle Realm, but they also roam all over the Lower Realm. They're invisible to non-tribers. Just wait till you see the city for the first time as a triber. Goblins are everywhere, but Times Square is just insane!"

Sy tried to imagine it, but couldn't.

The sky was dark and cloudy, and there were no stars. The guiding ray of green light lit the way and allowed them to see each other. This was reassuring; Sy was beginning to feel a little dizzy as their altitude increased.

"Where's the basecamp?" he asked.

"Location's secret and moves every month," said Xanthia. "Each tribe has their own basecamp, and none of us know where the others are, for security."

They moved through heavy cloud and Sy shivered, feeling cold. His ears hurt a little, too. How much longer would it take? The heavy substance they were moving through was dark.

Moments later he felt a deep, satisfying warmth penetrate his skin. They emerged from the dark thickness. Sy blinked in surprise; he was standing on solid ground and it was daylight! The sky was a penetrating violet, and an enormous bright star was shining down on him, invigorating his whole body. He stared down at his feet in amazement.

Ryder shared a smile with Raf and Xanthia. New recruits were always awestruck when they first entered the Middle Realm.

The landscape around Sy was blooming. What seemed like hundreds of species of flowers were blossoming at an accelerated rate. Shooting stars and sporadic multi-colored explosions filled the sky with brilliant color. Sy could make out shimmering mountains on the distant horizon.

It was a kaleidoscope.

Raf pointed to the giant star. "The Northern Star is the largest in the Middle Realm. It's like the sun but never moves from its position, guaranteeing that it is always daytime in the Middle Realm."

They took to the sky again, flying over the picturesque scene. Sy looked to the others. "I'm sorry I doubted you. This feels . . . right, somehow."

A dark shadow crossed the Northern Star. They looked up, startled. Ryder flew close and hovered beside Sy protectively. Two enormous bats were gliding above, their dark, scaled wings glistening—out of place against the beautiful backdrop. Riding on their backs, fixated on the four of them, were small, dark creatures with pointy ears and fluorescent red eyes. Sy strained to see properly. It looked like they weren't actually riding the bats, but connected to them in an unnatural way. As they came nearer, Sy saw that the creatures gripped a metal handlebar like a chopper motorcycle's that emerged from each bat's body. The metal curved around each bat's head and into its mouth.

"Dark elves," whispered Raf.

Sy could hear the fear in his voice.

Spurred on by the elves, the bats attacked, descending fast.

"Forcefield!" cried Ryder, Xanthia and Raf in unison, holding up their palms. A shimmering green barrier appeared, shielding the group, but the elves pulled out crossbows and shot arrows at them that looked to Sy to be powerful enough to penetrate anything. Sy caught a look of undisguised malice from the dark elves, which seemed to be directed at him personally, and saw Ryder frown as if he noticed it as well.

The forcefield held steady and the arrows ricocheted against its walls ineffectually. The elves retreated, looking furious.

"What are they?" Sy asked, his voice shaking.

"Dark elves," said Ryder. "Agents of the Darkforce."

"Scum of the universe," added Raf.

Xanthia was frowning. "What are they doing here?"

"What is the Darkforce?" Sy asked, not sure he wanted to hear the answer.

Xanthia's voice was low. "The Darkforce is the culmination of all the evil in the universe," she said.

"They seemed very interested in you!" Ryder said, nudging Sy. He glanced at Xanthia.

All trace of Xanthia's hesitation was gone. "This has never happened before. We need to get to basecamp and tell Taurus," she said.

The others nodded.

"Taurus is one of our Earth-tribe council representatives," Ryder told Sy.

"Look out!" screamed Raf.

The bats were bearing down on them with bombs of black liquid that smashed against the forcefield and ate into it like acid. The forcefield flickered and then extinguished. Sy closed his eyes instinctively, barely registering Ryder roughly grab his arm. Seconds later he was falling rapidly and felt himself hit the ground. He expected a bone-crunching thud, but there was no pain. He opened his eyes.

He was lying on his stomach, squeezed into a very small, dark space, and his first reaction was panic. He was just slightly relieved to have Ryder right beside him, tightly gripping his arm.

Xanthia and Raf had disappeared.

"Where are we? What happened?" he asked, the familiar choking feeling from being in a confined space coming over him. His heart rate increased and his breathing became rapid.

"I had no choice. They're definitely after you," whispered Ryder. "It's an Earth-tribe power; we can hide in our own shadows. I need to hold on to you to make sure you're also hidden. Raf and Xanthia have done the same."

"Will they find us?" Sy whispered fearfully, struggling to manage his claustrophobia.

"This is the first time I've had someone hide with me . . . stay quiet."

The dark elves scanned the area. Sy focused on controlling his breathing. Ryder seemed to be having a silent conversation; he was frowning and then nodding . . .

The elves hovered suspiciously, as if they knew Sy was right underneath them. Sy's mind was working overtime. Why were they after him? What had he done? He cringed at the steely resolve he saw in their malicious eyes. Ryder and Sy remained perfectly still. Sy's arm hurt, but Ryder did not relax his grip.

Sy heard a shout. Xanthia and Raf emerged from their hiding place and the elves urged the bats toward them.

"What are they doing?"

"Creating a diversion," said Ryder.

Xanthia and Raf let the dark elves get close before they accelerated to a giant tree, the bats in pursuit.

"Did they just disappear inside that tree?" asked Sy, forgetting to whisper.

"Earth-tribers can camouflage themselves with any natural earth substance. We can also teleport via trees," said Ryder.

The bats pulled up and the elves looked around, surprised their prey had disappeared. Xanthia and Raf teleported from tree to tree, disappearing and then emerging a good distance away. Sy watched them wrap their arms around the tree trunk and become invisible. They managed to infuriate and taunt the bats until, finally, the dark elves seemed to run out of ammunition and retreat.

Ryder and Sy stayed hidden, not sure if this was a trap. After tense moments, Ryder said it was safe for them to come out and, to Sy's immense relief, he was released from the confined space. Raf and Xanthia appeared on a tree branch about thirty feet up. They flew down to meet Sy and Ryder.

"That was close," said Raf, landing in front of them.

"Let's get out of here!" said Xanthia, looking shaken. She held up her palm. There was no talk as they flew quickly, guided by the green light, concentrating on getting Sy to camp safely.

Sy wasn't sure what to make of things. His mind wanted to reject it, but the more time he spent with Ryder and the others, the more obvious it was that he really was exposed to a secret world. He was deeply excited to witness their powers and knew he should be exhilarated that he'd been selected to join this world . . . but what was with those dark elves? It wasn't his imagination that he'd been singled out.

Why would anyone want to harm *him*? He knew nothing about being a triber. He looked around in awe as they flew through the Middle Realm, still stunned that this place existed!

Two enormous figures flew majestically in the distance, silhouettes against the beaming Northern Star. Wary, Sy instinctively slowed his pace.

"Our Protectors, patrolling Earth-tribe basecamp boundaries," said Xanthia. "They're Lions, the Grand Guard of the Zodiac Council," she explained. "They guard each tribe's basecamp and tribal events and can generate a unique energy forcefield for our protection that can be toxic, even fatal for intruders, including other tribers from Air, Fire or Water. They relocate the basecamp every month."

The Protectors moved with the grace of all the big cats and had huge wings. Their beautiful white coats were gleaming.

As they drew close, Sy saw other teenagers approaching. All new recruits received an escort on their first day, and they looked as nervous as he suddenly felt. The Protectors were watching them all carefully. At the entrance, Sy got an aerial view of the Earth-tribe basecamp.

It was an awesome sight! A series of colored tents—forest-green, red, orange, yellow, purple, midnight-blue and indigo—were dotted around a giant white tent. A flag with the Earth-tribe symbol flew from its topmost peak. It reminded Sy of a circus.

They landed and joined the line of tribers waiting to pass through the giant gates into camp. Sy approached cautiously, staying well behind the others. Two Lion Protectors had positioned themselves on either side of the entrance, their tails wrapped around their bodies. They were a lot more intimidating up close. Their pupils were green—Earth-tribe green.

Ryder held his palm up for inspection. "It doesn't hurt," he said to Sy.

Xanthia addressed one of the Protectors: "New recruit." She ushered Sy forward.

The Lion appraised him. Sy held up his palm, feeling slightly stupid. He had no idea what he was showing them. His palm tingled slightly, the lion gave a slight nod, and he was granted entry.

4

Earth-tribe Basecamp

As they moved toward the massive tent, Sy could feel his heart beating faster in anticipation of what lay ahead. Inside was even more imposing. He paused in the enormous foyer, convinced for a moment that he was floating in space. It was dimly lit, and clusters of stars, grouped as if in patterns, hovered in midair. Xanthia's face reflected the light from the stars as she looked up. "The constellations of the zodiac," she said.

The floor was white marble. Etched in the marble was an enormous circle, divided into twelve equal parts. On each of the parts was one of the twelve zodiac symbols. Sy studied them with great interest, his eye automatically moving to the bull, the symbol for his own star sign, the sign of Taurus. He had the distinct impression that this was a very important place, and that there was more to learn about the Middle Realm and being a triber than powers.

"This space helps remind us that light is projected

into our being from above and that there are greater forces at work, beyond our comprehension," said Xanthia.

Sy could see how serious she was; she was perfectly still and her blue eyes were dark and thoughtful. He fixed his eyes on the large moon floating above them—a luminous, perfect white circle. He could make out the outline of a bull in its center. Numbers and words floated underneath: fifteen days until the new moon.

"That's our lunar clock," said Xanthia. "It shows the passing of time according to the moon's cycle. It changes every day as it counts down to the next lunar festival. It's showing a full moon now, because that's when we get our new recruits, and when some tribers leave the tribe forever." She gestured to the clock. "The full moon is the middle of the lunar cycle. You can see the bull in the center of the moon because it's the lunar month of Taurus."

"Every month, tribers from all four tribes compete against each other at the lunar festivals, just like a giant sports meet," Ryder added. "We put our powers to use, learn to work in teams and push ourselves. The ultimate victory is winning the annual Lunar Championship at the end of the year."

"I'm going to find Taurus," said Xanthia.

Sy tried to take in everything he was seeing and being told. Taurus seemed like a strange name for a council leader. He was imagining a wise old man with a long white beard and wasn't sure how to act around such an important person. Ryder and Raf led him out of the foyer into a large room with lots of comfortable-looking couches and armchairs. He saw teenagers of different ages and nationalities, but no adults. New recruits were discernible by their anxious faces, but mostly the atmosphere was relaxed and laid back.

Raf scanned the room. "I'll go get Isobel," he said.

Sy, who was naturally shy with new people, felt completely overwhelmed and out of his depth. This was like being the new kid at school.

"Let's get a seat," said Ryder. "We'll hang with you until your initiation."

Sy felt a stab of anxiety, because initiation meant Ryder would be leaving soon. He'd been depending on the comforting presence of Ryder to get through whatever lay ahead.

"I'll meet up with you straight after, for your tour of the camp," Ryder reassured him.

Crossing the room, they were approached by all sorts of people wanting to talk to Ryder, many of them girls. Ryder was friendly and seemed genuinely interested in everyone. Sy had no choice but to follow, swallowing his nerves and breathing deeply to steady himself. Ryder sat them down at an empty table and pulled over some stools. "Sodas and fries, please," he said.

Sy looked around, wondering who he was talking to and hoping it wasn't him. Seconds later, the soda and fries appeared on the table. Sy shrugged to himself. Well, why not? It wasn't any more strange than anything else he'd seen in the Middle Realm. He helped himself to some golden fries and gratefully sipped his soda. The appetizers at Samuel's house felt like they'd happened in another lifetime.

Raf approached, accompanied by a girl. She had shoulder-length brown hair with bangs and large hazel eyes fringed with dark lashes. "Sy, meet Isobel." He grabbed two stools and sat down noisily.

"Welcome," she said, smiling at him.

Sy smiled back shyly.

"It's a lot to take in to begin with, but being a triber is très cool," she said.

Sy liked her French accent.

"We got attacked by dark elves on our way here," Raf told her.

Isobel looked shocked. "Mon dieu!"

Ryder and Raf went into detail about the ambush. Everyone had been told about the ongoing presence of the Darkforce, but no one they knew had encountered it personally. Isobel was firing questions at Ryder and Raf, to which they had no answers.

Sy withdrew deeper into his own anxious thoughts.

Xanthia sat down and helped herself to some fries. "I couldn't find Taurus," she said.

"There's no adults anywhere," Sy observed, slightly embarrassed to realize he'd spoken his thought aloud.

Isobel nodded. "That's right. Tribers are between thirteen and eighteen," she said. "When you reach eighteen, you leave after a special ceremony. Privileged tribers join the Tribal-elite after graduation; they never lose access to the Middle Realm."

Like Samuel, thought Sy.

Isobel ordered more fries. "We're divided into teams of five that compete in the monthly lunar festivals. The team leaders bring the new tribers to basecamp. It's not like school. Teams usually hang out together, despite the age differences."

"How old are you?" asked Sy.

"I'm fourteen. Ryder, Raf and Xanthia are fifteen," she said.

Sy was not so happy to be the youngest.

"Stick with us—we'll hook you up," Raf told him.

"Xanthia's your team leader. Raf is also in your team," said Isobel. "Ryder and me, we are together."

"In a team you mean," Raf teased.

Isobel blushed.

So, he wouldn't be in a team with Ryder. Sy stifled his disappointment, trying to absorb it all, but double-taking when he found out the festivals were held on the moon. Sy listened and watched. The others were excited about the upcoming festival, and so at ease with each other.

"Tribers come from every corner of the world," said Xanthia. "We only really get to know the Northern Hemisphere tribers. During our Lower Realm daytime, tribers from the Southern Hemisphere use the camp. We all get together at the end of the year in Lunar Pisces. I don't know how the Council does it. Here's Taurus."

Hundreds of tiny silver stars rained down from above and a hush fell over the room. Ryder, Xanthia, Isobel and many others rose and said their goodbyes. Xanthia gently patted Sy on the shoulder as they left. "You'll be fine," she said.

"It's all good," whispered Ryder.

Raf gave him a nod.

Moments later, a pair of sharp white horns appeared, followed by the large body of a bull with a glossy black coat. All the new recruits, Sy included, started in surprise and exchanged anxious looks. The bull was as black as night. It had beady eyes and a long tail.

There was a nervous silence. Taurus stood before them, scanning the room at the new faces. He smiled widely, displaying sharp teeth. "Welcome to you all," he said in an encouraging tone.

Sy could tell by the way many others were fidgeting that he wasn't the only one feeling anxious. Taurus was so . . . imposing.

"I am Taurus, member of the Zodiac Council and

founding father of the astrological sign of Taurus. Your destiny to join Earth-tribe was predetermined at the moment of your birth, based on the position of the planets and stars at that time. You were all born in the lunar month of Taurus, thirteen years ago."

This was Taurus, thought Sy. The real-life version of the sign he represented!

Taurus's eyes lingered on Sy. "Each person's zodiac sign determines the tribe they belong to," he said. "You are all linked astrologically by your distinctive Taurean traits."

Sy knew he could be stubborn at times, and once he had made his mind up on a matter, it was difficult, almost impossible, for anyone to change it.

"Virgo and Capricorn Earth-tribers will be initiated at a separate ceremony later in the year," Taurus announced. "Gemini, Libra and Aquarius belong to Air-tribe; Aries, Leo and Sagittarius are Fire-tribers, and Cancer, Scorpio and Pisces belong to the Water-tribe," he finished.

Taurus paused and looked around the room. "Now there are three rules that are of the utmost importance." His face became more serious, and his voice had a deep rumble that made the floor beneath them vibrate. "One: you can never reveal anything about the Middle Realm to non-tribers. Two: you must never discuss your basecamp's location with anyone, with the exception of your fellow Earth-tribers. Three: powers

31

are to be used with discretion. Intent to fatally injure another is forbidden." He paused for a moment.

"If you break any of these rules it will result in immediate expulsion from Earth-tribe and memory loss of this realm. You will also forfeit the chance to be selected as a triber in all future incarnations," he finished sternly.

It felt to Sy as if these instructions were being etched into his mind. A whispered murmur passed through the crowd: "Powers!"

Taurus relaxed his expression. "Use your time here to develop your natural abilities and honor your tribe. Tonight you commence on the path to your own truth. Your journey will evolve as you acquire knowledge. Each tribe celebrates the coming of the new lunar month. The moon changes in accordance with the moving planets, and this provides a learning opportunity," he said. "You all belong to a team and should look to your team leader for guidance. Train hard, and when you complete all seven levels you graduate and become Tribal-elite."

"How long does each level take to complete?" asked a girl next to Sy.

Sy admired her confidence.

"Levels 1 to 6 each take six lunar cycles. That's six months each," Taurus answered. "Tribers gain additional powers when each new level is completed. Level-7 takes twelve lunar cycles to complete. Those who are successful are granted a further twelve lunar cycles of advanced training before graduation, where they enjoy the use of all of their powers including traveling at light speed." Taurus drew himself up to eagerly announce, "The final phase of the initiation ceremony will now commence!"

Sy's nerves went into overdrive and he knew he wasn't alone. The new recruits seemed awed by all this information, and some were whispering among themselves. The room dissolved and they found themselves in a different space, circular and very white and sparse.

Taurus spoke in a low voice. "Our Earth-tribe symbol is now before you."

On the floor, a green circle appeared with two mountains inside it, the peaks close together as if they were embracing.

"In order to be formally initiated, you must connect your palm with the original source of all Earth-tribe power, located within the sacred Twin Peaks of Legov. Once you do this, you will be transported back here."

"Bloody brilliant!" whispered Sy's neighbor.

"Zak," he said, as Sy turned toward him. He had a clipped English accent, his dark hair was cropped short, and his green eyes complemented his coffee-colored skin. He held out his hand.

Sy shook it, shyly.

Taurus called each triber forward, and one by one

each new recruit stepped into the circle, only to emerge a few moments later smiling and looking invigorated.

Finally it was Sy's turn.

"Good luck," whispered Zak, next in line.

Sy hesitated. He took a small step forward and was encased in the green light.

5

The Nefiot Gnomes

Energized and blissful, Sy closed his eyes, savoring the feeling of the light pouring into him. When he opened them again, he was facing a great stone mountain. Sy was amazed at the contrasting landscape; to his right were rolling green hills and lush meadows that looked as if they went on for miles; on his left was a giant blue-white glacier. Behind him was a sandy desert.

Earth-tribe's symbol, engraved in stone at the base of the mountain, was glowing green. Sy placed his palm on the symbol as instructed and waited.

Rays of light traveled from his palm, up his arm and burst out of his body in every direction. He stared, mesmerized, but no sooner than it began, it was over. He felt an unexpected swell of pride: he had been initiated into Earth-tribe! He waited to be teleported back, as Taurus had advised.

Instead, a soft, female voice seemed to echo all around him. "Welcome Sy! We have long awaited your arrival. The Council has requested that you meet with the sacred Nefiot gnomes to hear important information related to your destiny . . ."

As soon as the words had been spoken, Sy was transported to a ledge of rock, jutting from the mountain. Two creatures bowed to him and, clumsily, he bowed back. They looked like identical twins, short with small black eyes and each of their long noses with a round fleshy tip at its end. Their cinnamon skin was heavily wrinkled, and they wore long white robes and had beards to match. They smiled at him warmly.

Sy looked down, uneasy. It was a steep drop. "Where am I?"

"Welcome to the land of Nef, Sy."

The gnomes spoke in unison. It was a little unnerving because he didn't know where to look.

"We are the Nefiot Gnomes, and we have been requested by the Zodiac Council to make you aware of certain matters," they said.

Perfect! thought Sy. Maybe now he'd hear something that would help him understand why those crazy dark elves had been after him.

"The Zodiac Council protects all creatures. Much of their time is spent trying to counteract and neutralize the negative energy that exists in the universe. This evil is called the Darkforce, and it is gaining strength, resulting in an unnatural shift in the balance of power between good and evil."

Sy found it hard to concentrate. How were they managing to speak at *exactly* the same time?

"Everyday occurrences in the Lower Realm—the greed, jealousy, hatred, selfishness and continued violence humans show toward one another—inspires the Darkforce and provides it with ammunition. The Darkforce is yet to unleash the full force of this negativity into the Lower Realm, but the possibilities are frightening . . ."

Remembering the malevolence in those fluorescent eyes, Sy felt his stomach clench in fear.

The Nefiot Gnomes nodded, as if understanding his feelings. "We have had disturbing reports that more and more people are having nightmares. By interfering with dreams, the Darkforce is stealing hope and causing despair. The Zodiac Council is on high alert . . ." The gnomes gave a slight bow, as if in deference. "It is the young people of the world who are the future, placing increased importance on the selection process for tribers. The Council is constantly scanning the Cosmic DNA to identify exceptional individuals who have a greater propensity for selflessness."

There was a short pause. Four pairs of eyes surveyed Sy kindly. "The Council has foreseen a significant event that has not yet occurred, where you, Sy, play a major role."

Me? thought Sy. He found it almost impossible to imagine that he had been singled out.

"The outcome of this event will greatly impact the future of the Lower and Middle Realms," continued the gnomes. "We bring it to your attention now because the Darkforce has an intricate spy network throughout both realms. Unfortunately, they also are aware of your importance. More urgently, they are threatened by your existence." The gnomes shook their heads slightly, as if in dismay. "They have already made an attempt on your life, which you have narrowly escaped."

Having his suspicions validated made Sy feel even worse.

"The Council has always watched over and protected you. It was imperative that you be initiated today, as this will provide you with even greater protection. It is also imperative that you understand: the Darkforce tried to prevent you from joining your tribe." The gnomes leaned forward, as if to press their point. "They are calculated, evil and thorough. You must remain on guard at all times. Trust your instincts . . ."

Full of questions, Sy opened his mouth, but before he could utter a word, he was back in the initiation room, face to face with Taurus. The great bull gave Sy a penetrating look and nodded, as if satisfied.

Sy felt about to burst with frustration. Why him? Why should *he* have to be the one they were after? Clearly unaware of Sy's anxiety, Zak clapped him on the shoulder and stepped excitedly onto the Earth-tribe symbol.

Sy wanted to understand more about what the gnomes had told him, but he didn't know who to ask. Taurus was much too imposing. He'd have to wait for Ryder.

Taurus addressed the group. "Your palm devices are now activated."

Sy looked down, as did the other new tribers. The Earth-tribe symbol embedded in his left palm was glowing.

"It is a universal navigation device which will provide you with directions anywhere. It will help you find our Earth basecamp wherever you are, and holds your tribal DNA." Taurus tossed his mighty head and stamped a hoof. "It's also a universal translator that allows you to communicate with all creatures across all realms, no matter what language they speak."

Everyone was inspecting his or her palms in fascination. Sy wished he could share Zak's enthusiasm, but he was consumed with the message of the Nefiot Gnomes, impatient to get back to Ryder.

Taurus continued: "From tomorrow, you will be teleported to Earth basecamp when you fall asleep at night and achieve the state of deep sleep known as Dreamtime." He beamed at them. "You will be transported back to your beds before sunrise and wake fully refreshed."

A group of tribers arrived, and Sy saw it included Xanthia and what looked like other team leaders; they stood proudly before Taurus, who acknowledged them with a wide smile. "And now it is time for your team leaders to show you around and allocate your new tribal birthdays."

"Why do we need a new birthday?" asked Zak.

"Your tribal birthday is a true reflection of your birth. The planets and stars were in a certain position at the exact moment you were born," Taurus answered. "This position is very relevant to who you are as an individual. According to the zodiac calendars, the date varies every year." He smiled. "You will find your energy levels are heightened on this day, and your powers intensified."

* * *

Back in the room off the main entrance, the team leaders were organizing the tour. Sy was pleased to discover that he and Zak would be together. Xanthia introduced him to the final member of his team, Brady, who was fourteen. He had dark hair and was very thin. He told them he was from Hong Kong.

Isobel and Ryder joined them too. His team didn't have any new team members that month, and Ryder wanted to see Sy's reaction when he got his first look at basecamp.

Sy's palm flashed. A message appeared, advising

that he only had an hour left in the Middle Realm; he stared at it, feeling weird, and it flashed off.

"You'll get used to it," said Ryder. "How was your initiation?"

"I need to talk to you," Sy whispered urgently. "When I —"

"Let's get going," Xanthia interrupted, clearly eager to start the tour.

Sy had no choice but to follow her to the main foyer, where he and Zak received their new birthdays on the Taurean section of the Zodiac Wheel.

They made their way outside. Xanthia walked purposefully and her voice was filled with pride. "Each camp has the same basic layout," she said. "The Lounge is over here." She led them to a huge tent. "This is where we hang out."

The Lounge had an awesome nightclub environment. French rap was belting out in the semi-darkness. The space was divided into sections with elevated private areas. There was a massive bar and dancefloor under an enormous crystal chandelier. Several DJs hovered midair.

"The vibe of the Lounge is always changing," Xanthia told them.

"The collective energy impacts on everything: lighting, décor and music," added Isobel.

Moments later, the room brightened, the music became more upbeat, and the walls changed from dark gray to crazy graffiti designs. The walls were spray-painting themselves with different colors and pictures.

"Bloody brilliant," said Zak.

Ryder waved to some tribers who were gesturing for him to join them. "Later," he promised Sy, and headed over to them.

Sy wanted to wait and see if the room would change into another mood while they were there, but Xanthia ushered them out. "Over there are the training tents." She pointed to seven large tents, each a different color.

Raf followed her lead. "The color of the tent reflects the training level you're up to," he said. "You two will begin at the red tent, Level-1. Training is optional, but we all do it to improve our skills and enhance our powers. If you don't graduate at Level-7 you are banished from the tribe forever. You need to complete all levels to qualify for Triber-elite status. Not everyone makes it through."

Xanthia gestured to an area to their left. "Everyone has their own personal tent, which is your private space."

Ryder rocked up and gave him a playful shove. "There's also the Entertainment tent where we can play all the latest games." He grinned. "Any game you want—just ask and it'll appear."

Zak's face lit up. "That's ace!"

"They're a little different to the games in the

Lower Realm," said Ryder, grinning at Zak's enthusiasm. "They're the future versions."

Sy made a mental note to continue his campaign to get a computer in his room. He was going to need serious practice or he'd be left behind!

They followed Xanthia to another tent. "This is the Knowledge tent," she said. "A learning area where you can get information on anything."

Ryder pointed. "And over there are a dozen virtual reality suites where you can create adventures or live out your greatest desires," he said.

Isobel blushed, and Sy wondered if her "greatest desire" had something to do with Ryder.

Winding up the tour, Xanthia turned to Sy and Zak. "Let me know if I can help you with anything. I'm really looking forward to getting to know you better," she said warmly.

Raf grinned. "Lucky you landed in the A-team."

Isobel held up her hand. "Your palms are about to give you the one-minute warning," she said.

Large numbers covered his palm and Sy stared. From the first appearance of fifty-nine, it was counting down: now forty-nine, forty-eight . . . Sy joined in the quick goodbyes. "See you, Zak. Bye, Ryder, Raf, Isobel —" Nineteen, eighteen . . . "Thanks, Xanthia!"

Three, two, one . . .

6

I.N.C.

Sy awoke with a start. He lay still, his eyes closed, re-living the Middle Realm. Was it all just a really intense dream? There was a lot to be excited about, but Sy also felt uneasy . . . he hadn't had a chance to dis-cuss the warning from the Nefiot Gnomes with Ryder. His stomach tightened and he looked around his room, feeling paranoid that dark elves might appear any minute. He couldn't help the flare of resentment that he was now burdened with having to worry about his safety.

There was also the small matter of keeping the Middle Realm a secret from his parents. How was anyone supposed to keep such a giant part of their life a secret? Sy had his moments with his parents, like all teenagers, but he'd always been pretty honest with them . . . and Rebecca wasn't the easiest person to lie to.

Sitting up, he looked around carefully. Everything

seemed the same; his clothes were strewn on the floor where he'd left them, and he was wearing his pajamas. He jumped up and did a quick check to see that all of him was awake and out of bed.

He pulled open the colonial shutters to reveal a bright, sunny morning. Just yesterday he'd been looking forward to his dad's movie screening and preoccupied with the upcoming ballgame. Now everything had changed. How was he ever going to get through his days when he had nights to look forward to?

What would people at school say if he told them that there was a parallel universe filled with myth-ical creatures, and teenagers with powers living a dual existence in complete secret? Despite his reservations, there was no denying that the Middle Realm was awesome! Earth-tribe basecamp was mind-blowing, a fantasy come to life.

He strained his ears to see if he could hear his parents moving around the townhouse, but all was quiet. Once his dad was up, Trent would get them fresh bagels like he did every Saturday morning. Sy guessed his dad was probably wiped out; the last few months of getting the movie ready had been pretty intense. Sy's stomach grumbled. He sighed; he couldn't wait another minute—he'd have to settle for granola.

He was about to go in search of food when a pixie's face, hovering over his bed, scared him half to death.

"Welcome to Galaxy Connect," she chanted from

under her blonde crew cut. "All tribers must sign in to activate their I.N.C. account."

Her eyes registered Sy's confused expression. "Your *inter-realm network communicator*," she said slowly, enunciating each word.

"Huh?"

"Read the user manual," she said, sounding bored. A clear screen appeared beside the pixie's face. Sy's name and tribe appeared in bold letters with a list of terms of use. "Sign to activate, please," she said. "Thank you."

"I don't have a pen," said Sy, feeling stupid.

She rolled her eyes. "Not required. Hold up your left palm and press it on the screen. Tribal ID acts as your signature and your palm-print as your password."

Sy did as he was told.

"Thank you, sir. Your personal I.N.C. has been activated. Have a great day."

She disappeared and Ryder's face appeared instead. "Hey, Sy, finally. I've been trying you all morning, waiting for them to activate your I.N.C."

Sy was not as freaked out to see Ryder's face in midair as he would have been yesterday. "What is the I.N.C.?" he asked.

"It's a total comms system," Ryder said enthusiastically. "The I.N.C. connects all creatures of the Middle and Lower realms, twenty-four seven. It replaces your cell, Skype, and Facebook—it's like your computer,

TV, Internet, email, instant messaging, instagram, postal and courier delivery service all in one . . . it even has storage facilities. But the best thing —?"

"Wow." Sy poked ineffectually at the screen. "What do I do?"

"It's free, unlimited usage and all voice activated! Any time you want to speak to any triber, just say their name. Talk to as many people as you want, no file or data size limits."

"That's incredible."

"You think *that's* good," said Ryder. "If you want to send anything—any physical item—it gets delivered instantly."

"No way! How?"

"Didn't they explain *anything* when you signed up?"

"Not really."

"Just say 'I.N.C.', then touch what you want to send and say who you want to send it to. I'll give you a demo." Ryder held up a bagel. "I.N.C.—bagel to Sy Middleton, Earth-tribe!"

A little mailbox icon flashed in front of Sy. He reached in and grabbed a fresh bagel with sesame seeds on the top. "How did you know I was hanging for one of these?" He took a large bite. It was still warm.

"It's the only way to stay in contact with tribers in the Lower Realm during the day." Ryder took a bite of his own bagel and then talked with his mouth full.

"I speak to Xanthia and Raf on it all the time, although now we're learning to communicate telepathically. He's in LA and Xanthia's in Toronto. And the best part? It's completely invisible to non-tribers."

Sy attacked his bagel with another giant bite. The whole thing was totally awesome.

"So what did you think of the Middle Realm?" asked Ryder.

"Incredible."

"You're so lucky Xanthia's your team leader —"

Sy interrupted him. "Hey, I never got to tell you what happened at my initiation." He filled Ryder in on what the Nefiot gnomes had said. When he shared that the dark elves had definitely tried to sabotage his initiation, Ryder's lips tightened.

"I knew it!"

"What am I going to do?" asked Sy, anxiously.

"Watch your back for a start," said Ryder. "And hope the Council knows what it's doing."

Sy grimaced. He hardly felt reassured. Why couldn't the Darkforce be looking for someone else? "It's hard to believe all that stuff about being special," he admitted.

Ryder didn't say anything.

"I'm meant to be involved in some future event," said Sy. "Any ideas on what it could be?"

"Honestly . . . not really," replied Ryder, realizing he wasn't being very helpful.

Sy heard footsteps. "I've gotta go."

"Later," said Ryder, and disappeared from view.

* * *

Sy spent a lazy morning channel-surfing the TV while his parents re-lived the previous evening. His dad was still on a high. A few hours later he joined them for a jog in Central Park. Trent tried to convince them to do the shorter route near Tavern on the Green, but his mom insisted they do the five-mile route that took them through the lower section of the park.

In the park, Sy became anxious. He thought he caught sight of some dark elves but wasn't sure if his eyes were playing tricks on him. He nearly jumped out of his skin and lost his footing when a shadow loomed behind him.

It was Trent, trying to keep up!

Sy felt a stab of guilt. His parents would not be happy to know he was being hunted by the Darkforce, and even less happy that he'd kept it from them.

In the afternoon, Trent was going to visit Samuel Ryderson to go over some financials, and Sy offered to join him, hoping to see Ryder.

* * *

Samuel looked as distinguished as ever. He welcomed them warmly. "I'm sorry, Sy," he said. "Ryder's out with friends."

Disappointed, Sy busied himself with his dad's iPad until Samuel sent him into the kitchen for snacks. On his way, Sy passed framed pictures on the wall. Many of them were Samuel with very important-looking people, including past presidents. He stopped at one in particular: Samuel with a beautiful woman with caramel-colored eyes. Her face was painted like a warrior's and she held a spear. He wondered who she was.

In the kitchen, Sy opened the enormous subzero fridge, marveling at how much food there was for only two people: cold meats, a large quiche, a tray of lasagna, three different salads, dips, a baked cheese-cake and a giant fruit platter. Ryder must have an amazing appetite.

Samuel joined him just as he pulled out the cheese-cake. As Sy closed the fridge, he saw another cheesecake appear in the empty space.

"Great choice," said Samuel, eyeing the cake and turning on a fancy-looking coffee maker. He pulled out plates and forks and handed them to Sy. Samuel's faded turquoise eyes were twinkling. "You've had an interesting twenty-four hours," he said.

"I'm still in shock, I think," Sy admitted. "I feel like a target, and I don't know how I will keep this from my parents." He surprised himself with his frank admission. Even if Samuel was Triber-elite, Sy wasn't usually so forthcoming with his feelings.

"Of course, that's only natural," Samuel agreed. He looked steadily into Sy's eyes and, instantly, Sy felt calmer. His worry dissolved and he felt he had nothing to fear.

What had just happened?

He was about to ask, but Trent joined them and Sy was distracted by sharing large helpings of the delicious cake while Samuel entertained them with stories from the past.

Later, Sy went with his parents to Yankee Stadium to watch the Yankees play. Since he'd left Samuel's, he felt much more in control, although he found himself counting down the hours until he could see his new friends again.

As soon as he could, he was showered and in bed. He lay there for a while, unable to fall asleep. He began worrying that he wouldn't be able to reach the state of deep sleep required to make it to basecamp. Without Ryder and Xanthia, the Middle Realm seemed unattainable . . .

* * *

Sy was in Dreamtime, lying on the Taurean symbol on the Zodiac circle in the main entrance. Jumping up, he looked around, hoping to spot a familiar face. All around, other tribers were appearing on the circle. A few smiled at him before they headed off. He couldn't remember where to go.

Now was as good a time as any to try his new device. "I.N.C.—Josh Ryderson, Earth-tribe," he said, hopefully.

Ryder's face appeared. "Hey, Sy," he said. "I'm in the Lounge—through the main entrance and turn right."

The drapes of the Lounge swung open automatically, and Sy entered apprehensively. He could hear lots of noise and laughter, and it seemed as if everyone inside was in great spirits. The Lounge was more upbeat than it had been the previous night; it was pretty dark, with loud, thumping music. Ryder, sitting in one of the elevated sections with Xanthia, Raf, Brady and Isobel, waved him over.

"Sorry I missed you today," he said. "You should have told me you were coming."

"Your grandfather is awesome," said Sy.

"I know."

"Did you get here okay?" asked Xanthia, smiling at him in a friendly way. Her sky-blue shirt matched her eyes—and her mini-skirt revealed long, thin legs. Her blonde hair was loose, framing her face.

"Yeah," said Sy, looking away so no one would think he was staring. "Thanks."

He sat down next to Raf, who was having an intense discussion with Isobel about his favorite topic: the Argentinian soccer team. Raf's dad was born in Argentina, but he'd moved to LA to marry Raf's mom.

"We've won the World Cup twice, in '78 and '86. I've watched the reruns of the '86 game, and Maradona is a legend! Have you ever seen him play?"

"Yes, I've seen him." Isobel grinned at Xanthia and rolled her hazel eyes.

Raf gave him a nod. "What about you, Sy?"

"I'm more of a baseball and NFL fan."

"I'll send you some games to watch on the I.N.C.," said Raf enthusiastically. "You'll change your mind when you watch real football."

Sy found himself tuning into Xanthia telling Isobel about a date she'd been on, and he wasn't the only one listening; Ryder also seemed intrigued. And no wonder! The guy she was talking about was Dax Hunter—one of the most famous movie stars on the planet. Dax Hunter was a triber? It had never crossed Sy's mind that celebrities could be tribers.

Xanthia let out a long sigh. "I should've realized sooner that he's a total player. The private jet to Cannes was way over the top, but it was so cool . . . the Cannes Film Festival! We were hanging out with heaps of other celebs . . . until he expected me to hook up with him, and when I wouldn't, he turned nasty."

"Bastard." Isobel fiddled with her drink. "You know I was completely jealous," she said.

"Of what? I thought he'd be different with me, but I'm no one's groupie," said Xanthia firmly.

"His ego is out of control," said Isobel. "LB's also."

Sy couldn't believe it. Everybody knew LB and Dax were close friends—he was as famous as Dax!

"I won't make that mistake again," Xanthia promised.

Sy spotted Zak, looking around. He seemed unsure, so Sy left the table to get him. "Thanks, mate," said Zak gratefully.

Back at the table, Zak sat down looking nervous. Before he had a chance to say anything, Raf bombarded him with questions about soccer. Zak was from the UK, and it turned out he was mad about Manchester United. He and Raf got into a very technical discussion.

Isobel looked at her watch. "Let's go, Ryder—team training," she said, and ushered him possessively out of the Lounge.

Sy caught the amused look between Raf and Xanthia. "What level is Isobel?" he asked.

"Level-4," Xanthia said. "Ryder, Raf and I are Level-5. Each completed level gives you new skills and earns us a color in the light spectrum. When all seven colors are completed, we can travel anywhere at light speed."

"I can't wait," said Zak.

"Well, good, because Sy and Zak, it's time for your first training session in the red tent," Xanthia said. "Do you remember the way?"

"I think so," said Zak. As they left, Sy thought

how lucky he was to have him to share the experience with.

There were already a few people inside, huddled uncertainly, but the tent filled up quickly. There were no tables, chairs or desks, just standing room and a few stools. A tall, skinny creature entered and a hush fell. He had four fingers, four toes on his bare feet and a tail that swished on the floor as he walked. Sy wondered if he was a kind of troll.

"Hello to our newest recruits. My name is Nudd." The creature smiled kindly. "Today is the first of your training sessions to prepare you for the lunar festivals. I'm sure you will all do very well," he said. "You begin your journey with us at Level-1. Training units include Middle Realm Cultures, where you'll learn the history and customs of all who live here."

Nudd's tail swished from side to side. "Power Utilization is another unit. There, you'll be taught to use your powers effectively. Your basic powers as a new triber include: flying, navigation, sonar ability, generating forcefields, and martial arts. All tribers receive these powers when their DNA is enhanced."

The excitement in the room was palpable.

"Your new powers also include increased brain capacity," Nudd told them. "The average human only uses five percent of their conscious brain. When you reach Level-7 at seventeen, you will be using one hundred percent of your brain. Everything you do will be improved, and your new photographic memories will help you with school work in the Lower Realm."

Sy looked around. By the look of things, he wasn't the only one who was thrilled by this news. But there was more.

"When you complete Level-1, you'll have black belts in Kung Fu, Karate and Jujitsu, as well as longitude and latitude comprehension for navigation when flying—plus sonar abilities similar to bats and dolphins!" Nudd told them. "You will need to practice and be committed to master these new skills."

"Do all tribers have the same powers?" asked Zak.

Nudd smiled knowingly. "Powers vary based on the tribe you belong to. You will learn more about Earth-tribe powers as you progress. They include: Shadow Concealment, Tree Teleporting and Earth Blend."

"What about the other tribes?" asked Zak.

"Fire-tribers can create and control fire, and communicate with it." Nudd told them. "Air-tribers have advanced flying abilities. They can control the weather and communicate with flying creatures. Water-tribers can communicate with marine life, breathe underwater and control the use of water."

Everyone was awe-struck at how cool the powers were and started talking excitedly among themselves. Nudd floated off the ground and hovered above them. That got everyone's attention!

"The only way to become skilled is practice.

And, so, we begin immediately." Nudd lined them up on one side of the tent, keeping space between them. "Your forcefield is used to protect you from harm. It's invisible to non-tribers and can be used anywhere," he said. "The forcefield is generated from your palm, using light. Visualize the forcefield surrounding you and the area you want to protect. Then silently instruct the forcefield to appear—this is what we call a thought command."

It was not as easy as it sounded. The new tribers had trouble synchronizing the thought command and the light from their palms. Random beams of green light flew across the room.

"Now don't get discouraged," Nudd told them. "It'll take time to get it right, and then it will be seamless."

Sy was concentrating hard but could not get the light to surround him. The session was almost over, and Zak had not had much luck either. His face was screwed in deep concentration, and then, finally, with his last attempt, his thought command and the light aligned and he was surrounded by a green aura. It covered him from head to toe.

"Well done!" Nudd exclaimed.

"How did you do it?" asked Sy, a little envious.

"I really focused and then it just happened," Zak said, clearly thrilled. "Don't worry, mate, you'll do it next time," he added reassuringly.

After the training session, Sy and Zak met Raf and Ryder in the Entertainment tent. Sy and Ryder teamed up against Raf and Zak, and played a new video game not yet released in the Lower Realm. They were fiercely competitive. Ryder was a pro, but so was Zak. Sy knew he was letting the team down, but Ryder never once made him feel bad about it. In the end, Zak got his team over the line.

"Bloody brilliant!" he exclaimed happily, high-fiving Raf.

Their palms flashed with the one-minute warning.

"Rematch tomorrow," Ryder told them.

7

The Vision

Over the next week, Sy adjusted to the reality of being part of two very different worlds. There was school, baseball and other Lower Realm pursuits, and then there was the adrenalin rush of the Middle Realm. The hardest part was keeping it from his parents. A few times he'd been about to share something that had happened and stopped himself just in time. It didn't feel natural to Sy that Trent and Rebecca were oblivious to his new world—a week ago they'd been completely involved in every detail of his life!

But it certainly had its upside. Since becoming a triber, Sy had way more energy. His mind was sharper and his school grades were already improving. He was faster, stronger and better at everything. These changes did not go unnoticed by Rebecca.

"You seem happy," she commented one morning.

"Yeah, Mom, I am," he said, giving her a hug and wishing he could share more.

"Is there anything new happening at school?"

"Not really, but I'm late." He kissed her quickly on the cheek and bolted out the door before she could ask him anything else.

Ryder and Samuel were another highlight. Trent's movie was not only getting a lot of positive feedback from the scientific community, but gaining mainstream support and getting amazing publicity: Trent was scheduled to appear on *Good Morning America* the following week. His dad was already in discussion with Samuel about the finance for the next project, and the two families were spending time together. Besides the project, Samuel had sampled one of Rebecca's gourmet meals and was hooked. It helped Sy enormously that at least one of his new friendships could be shared with his parents.

* * *

Xanthia wasted no time in getting them started on preparations for the upcoming lunar festival. "Tribers are passionately committed to participating in the festivals," she said. "You'll notice there's a lot of rivalry between the teams." She looked pointedly at Raf.

He grinned. "What can I say? Our reputations are at stake!"

"How do they choose who's going to compete?" asked Zak.

"One team from each tribe is selected by the

Ringmaster," said Xanthia. "At the end of the Zodiac year, in the month of Lunar Pisces, Tribers compete individually in challenges against their own level, and all the teams compete in team events until there is one champion team."

Over the next weeks of training, Raf kept urging Sy to practice. He was encouraging, and surprisingly gentle. "You play a soccer ball with your feet, head and chest," he explained. "To score goals, your body needs to be in complete alignment. It's the same with creating a forcefield. You need to align thought and vision."

* * *

Back in the Lower Realm, it was just an ordinary school night. Sy was meant to be finishing his homework, but he was distracted by thoughts of all his new powers. He couldn't wait to learn how to teleport from tree to tree. He felt tempted to I.N.C. Zak but thought better of it: the sooner he finished his schoolwork, the sooner he could get to sleep and be in the Middle Realm.

* * *

Sy was alone in a dimly lit, circular room. As his eyes adjusted, he saw colored bubbles rising from the floor: green, red and white. He watched curiously as they rose, popped and vanished. He looked around for someone to explain, but he was on his own.

61

The bubbles slowly circled his head. Was something moving inside them? He focused his energy on one enormous red bubble that had begun to rise. The blurred image inside it became clearer and more in focus, and Sy felt a sudden, desperate need to see what was happening.

It was some kind of scene, set in the countryside, empty except for a lone figure that Sy couldn't quite make out. With a shock, he realized the shadowy dark edges of the landscape were moving: a sludge-like black lava was creeping in, attacking the ground surface, almost like it was contaminating it. Bubbling aggressively, it claimed more and more land with each passing second, until all that remained was an island where the petrified figure stood alone, frantically searching for an escape.

The image rotated toward Sy, zooming in closer and closer. Whoever it was, he was trying to communicate with Sy . . . to show him something. Sy leaned forward eagerly, but he could only see the guy's silhouette. The image resolved into a close-up of an outstretched palm holding an ornate, golden device with elaborate symbols. It zoomed back out, and with a sudden, sickening gush, the swirling pool of liquid tar swamped the tiny island, swallowing up the desperate scream for help that pierced Sy to the core.

* * *

He woke up face down on the Taurus symbol at Earth-tribe basecamp and lay there, his breathing uneven, trying to work out what had just happened. He stood up, feeling completely shaken, and found himself face to face with Taurus.

"Come with me."

Sy had no choice but to follow. He couldn't catch his breath and felt sick to his stomach. He kept going over the image he'd seen, surprised to feel such deep anguish at the loss of a faceless stranger. It was as if there was some weird connection between him and the guy in the bubble. A fear clutched at him: what if it was Ryder?

Taurus led him into a beautiful room with decorative furniture and plush, velvet drapes. Portraits of legendary Earth-tribers hung on the walls in golden frames. Sy sat in a leather armchair and faced the Earth-tribe leader expectantly.

Taurus spoke quietly and came straight to the point. "Sy, tonight you have dreamed of your brother."

Sy's mind totally flipped. "What are you on about?" he asked.

"You have been an only child, but the time is now right for you to know the truth. The young man in your dream does exist, and he is your brother. Your souls are joined, and his destiny is intricately linked to yours—to the future event the Nefiot Gnomes warned you about at your initiation."

"But my mom and dad —" Sy blurted, wrestling with a painful rush of disbelief and betrayal.

"Are unaware of his existence," said Taurus gently.

"How is that possible?"

"Things are exactly as they must be."

Was Taurus kidding? That wasn't good enough. Sy cursed in his mind and clenched his fists in frustration. Was Taurus deliberately tormenting him?

"Can I see him?" Sy pleaded.

"I am sorry, Sy, but no," said Taurus, gently but firmly. "You are in danger from the Darkforce and your brother is too, even more than you. A meeting between you could have grave consequences. Rest assured he is under our protection."

He didn't *look* under your protection, thought Sy furiously. "Where is he?"

"That must be kept secret, for safety rea—"

"But my vision!" Sy interrupted forcefully, desperate to know where they were keeping his brother. "He's in trouble. He needs help now! He was trying to show me something . . ."

"Sy, you will have to trust me that your brother is safe . . . for the moment."

But Sy was not reassured. On the contrary, he was furious. He needed to be alone to think, not in this room being watched so closely by Taurus. He was pretty sure that Taurus could read his thoughts, and he resented the intrusion. And yet somehow, although it was crazy, he knew Taurus was telling him the truth: he had a brother! He stood up as the enormity of this realization sank in.

Taurus's serious face was kind. "Sy, this is a lot for you to take in. Always remember that the universe has its own agenda for us, and human desires and divine timing are sometimes not aligned. But it is the divine timing that ultimately has our best interests at heart."

Sy nodded, not really listening. He just wanted to get out of there and find Ryder. "Can you tell me his name at least?" he asked resentfully.

Taurus was silent for a few moments. "It is Gabriel," he said quietly.

Sy nodded. "I have to go to training," he said, and Taurus let him go.

He didn't go to training. He went straight to his personal tent and I.N.C.'d Ryder. "Can you meet me here?" he asked.

"Don't you have training? Hey, are you all right, Sy?" Ryder asked. "You look trashed."

"Hurry," said Sy.

Ryder arrived and Sy told him everything. They sat for a while, not speaking.

"Ryder, I've got to find him," said Sy fervently, breaking the silence.

"How?" asked Ryder. "You don't even know what he looks like."

"I don't care. I have to find a way," insisted Sy.

"He came to me for a reason. He needs me . . . Gabriel." His voice broke.

"Sy, I'll help you find your brother," promised Ryder. "But you also have to focus on everything else you've been told. The Nefiot Gnomes and the Council are serious. It's critical that you watch your back. Remember the dark elves!"

Sy nodded, feeling dazed.

"You can't say anything to your parents about your brother," Ryder warned, accurately reading Sy's thoughts. "Taurus said they don't know anything anyway. And if you do, you'll be expelled. They'll wipe your memory. You won't even remember he exists. The smartest thing to do is find out as much as you can without jeopardizing your status as a triber."

Ryder was right, but Sy couldn't just do nothing. "I'll never rest until I find Gabriel," he said stubbornly.

* * *

Sy felt a new sense of purpose when he joined Xanthia, Zak and the rest of his team for their strategy session. Now that he was committed to finding his brother and Ryder had agreed to help, he allowed himself a small frisson of excitement at the thought that he had a sibling. Gabriel, Gabriel; he kept repeating the name in his mind as if it could draw his brother to him.

Xanthia was sharing her views on where she felt

the team needed to focus. "We should continue practicing our combined forcefield. We're only as strong as our weakest link. And I need to do more work on my telepathy skills."

She was worried. Sy could hear the stress in her voice.

"Relax!" said Raf, putting his arm around her. "We're doing great. You're an awesome leader."

She smiled at them, a little self-conscious. "Sorry, I get kind of wound up sometimes."

They practiced their combined forcefield, overlapping their individual fields to increase its strength. After only a few attempts, Zak's was perfect.

"Bloody brilliant!" said Raf, in a really bad English accent. The entire group laughed.

He could not concentrate. His brother would not get out of his mind.

"Let's take some time out for a bit of one-on-one," suggested Raf. "What do you think, Xanthia? I'll see if I can bring Sy here up to speed." He winked at Sy.

They broke into two groups, and Sy immediately felt the pressure was off.

He put his hand on Sy's shoulder. "You're *overthinking it*! You've got to *visualize* the forcefield and let that be your *only thought*—just for that moment. Trust in yourself. You're strong enough to do it, Sy. Probably stronger than you know. So come on, clear your mind and go for goal."

Sy relaxed his shoulders, controlled his breathing and let everything—even Gabriel—fade into the background. He visualized and poured his intention into the thought.

"That's more like it," said Raf.

"Awesome!" said Sy, eager to try again.

Thanks to Raf's patience, within the hour his forcefield was perfect: seamless, strong and fast.

"Thanks, Raf," Sy said gratefully.

"No sweat," he answered.

The team got back together and tried the combined forcefield again. Xanthia was beaming, and Sy could only agree with Zak: bloody brilliant! He was feeling pretty good when he and Zak headed off to Cultural Studies.

Sy liked learning about the different cultures of the Middle Realm. He couldn't believe so many different types of mythical creatures existed.

"There are many species of elves, and most are good," Nudd told them, swishing his tail. "The dark elves are the ones to watch out for. They have a history of violence and aggression, as well as powerful evil magic," he warned. "If you encounter a dark elf, it's best to avoid him rather than take him on."

Sy realized just how lucky he was to have gotten away from them the night he was initiated.

* * *

On a warm afternoon a few days later, Sy and Ryder were studying at Ryder's place while Trent and Samuel went over some business. Sy couldn't concentrate. He'd become obsessed with the idea of finding his brother, but had no clue where to start.

"Did you hear that some other tribers were attacked on initiation night?" Ryder said.

"No," said Sy, surprised.

"Dark elves again. The Council is on high alert. This sort of thing has never happened before."

The elevator opened and Trent stepped out. "How's the studying?" he asked.

"All right," said Sy, feeling a bit weird. Finding out about Gabriel had really topped up his guilt quota. He wasn't exactly lying to his dad about studying, but he wasn't exactly telling the truth, either.

"I've got to meet your mom," Trent said. "Samuel has invited you to stay for dinner, so we'll come back later, if that suits."

Sy was thrilled. "Cool," he said.

Shortly after, Ryder said, "We need snacks." He pushed back his laptop. "To help inspire creative thinking," he added, stretching.

They raced down the stairs to the kitchen. Samuel was there, sipping an espresso and reading the *New York Times*. He looked up, smiling, as he always did when he saw his grandson.

"Hungry?" he asked, looking at them knowingly.

"I got a fresh batch of the chocolate chubbies you like from Chelsea Market," he told Sy. "I've added them to the auto-refill."

Sy thanked him, thinking for the hundredth time how cool Samuel was and how happy he was that Ryder had such an awesome grandfather.

"But then it's back to the books," Samuel instructed them firmly. He was easygoing about most things but very strict where Ryder's education was concerned. Study was always put first. Sy's parents agreed whole-heartedly with this attitude, and that meant they were supportive when Sy asked to spend time with Ryder.

The best thing about Samuel was that he was Triber-elite. You could be honest with him about the Middle Realm, and he was more than willing to give advice on how to excel at training and enhancing powers. Sy wished he could tell him about Gabriel and get his advice, but given he was deliberately going against Taurus by looking for him, he decided it wasn't the best idea.

Ryder poured freshly squeezed orange juice for himself and Sy from a beautiful glass pitcher. "You said you'd tell me more about Incubus," Ryder reminded his grandfather.

The Nefiot Gnomes had mentioned Incubus and his connection with the Darkforce on his initiation. Sy felt a lump of fear in his stomach.

"Just briefly, and then it's back to the books, Joshua,"

said Samuel, putting down his paper and giving Ryder and Sy his full attention.

"It was about a thousand years ago that Incubus, a very powerful sorcerer skilled in dark magic, stole the *Book of Dreams* from the Sleep Custodians and —"

"What's the *Book of Dreams*?" interrupted Sy.

"The *Book of Dreams* was invented by the Sleep Custodians to record a copy of every person's dreams," said Samuel.

"Why did they want to collect people's dreams?" asked Sy.

"To help people recall them, so they could learn from the important messages they contain," Samuel explained. "Dreams are powerful. If we were able to remember and understand our dreams, we'd have a greater insight into ourselves when we're awake. Incubus, or the Dream Sorcerer as he's been known since, stole the book." Samuel finished his coffee and reached for the orange juice. "After a while, he began tampering with the dreams, converting them into nightmares. He steals hope, and fills the world with despair. The imbalance is having a global impact."

"How does he *get* the dreams?" asked Sy.

"He uses an army of enslaved dream-catchers, the dream demons, to steal the dreams and deliver them to the book."

Sy was greatly intrigued. "How do you know about dream demons?"

"I've seen one first hand," answered Samuel.

Sy was impressed.

"A Sleep Custodian warrior and I once tailed a dream demon who'd just stolen a friend's dream. We didn't get very far, though, and lost the trail." Samuel sighed and rose from his seat. "Now, enough about the Dream Sorcerer. You've each got an essay to finish," he said firmly.

8

The Four Winds

Summer had finally hit the city; it was warm in the shade. Sy's class was walking to the Guggenheim on an excursion. As they headed along Fifth Avenue toward Eighty-Ninth Street, Sy was alert and on the lookout for any type of threat. The warning from the Nefiot Gnomes, as well as Ryder's insistence that he watch his back, had penetrated his psyche. He no longer felt safe, particularly in the Lower Realm.

A red double-decker sightseeing bus passed them, doing the uptown loop, a group of goblins gesturing loudly from the top deck as they raced across the seats, climbing over the oblivious Lower Realm passengers. A goblin wearing a Yankees baseball cap stood on the tour guide's head and, to the delight and great amusement of the others, copied his every move. "Next stop: Guggenheim," he mimicked wildly. The others cheered so loudly that Sy couldn't believe no one else could see or hear them.

His school group arrived at the museum and headed toward the Sackler Center for Arts Education. Sy was looking forward to the exhibition that featured paintings and sculptures by well-known Aboriginal artists from Central Australia.

Their guide was brisk in her tailored black suit and very high heels. She shook hands with Sy's teacher and addressed the class, patting her dark hair, which was pulled back in a tight chignon. "Australian Aboriginal culture is one of the oldest civilizations on earth," she said. "Of course, there are diverse cultural customs among the various Indigenous Australian nations."

She moved their group toward a series of paintings. "Before white settlers, Aboriginal people lived off the land, continually moving to give it time to heal. Their wisdom teaches that if you exhaust the resource, it will be unable to provide for you next time."

"Wow," thought Sy. How different was that attitude to the way most humans lived on earth: plundering the planet and abusing the oceans until it looked like there'd soon be nothing left. He was so proud of his dad for at least taking a stand.

"Aboriginal art both creates a bond with and expresses the importance of *the Dreaming*." Their guide adjusted her designer glasses. "The stories are creation stories, crucial in shaping relationship to the land and connection to all living things."

Sy looked at the dotted motifs and intricate designs.

Their guide steered them to another room of the exhibition. "You will see that this series of artworks differs greatly from the work we have just viewed. Here we see an early settler interpretation of a traditional Aboriginal setting."

Her voice faded away. Sy's attention had been caught by paintings hanging on a wall to his left. He hung back as his classmates dutifully filed past. These were not abstract and symbolic like the work they'd seen so far, and depicted scenes of traditional Indigenous culture.

Sy looked closely. Women and children were clapping, as men carrying spears, with faces and bodies painted, danced around a fire. Kangaroos and emus walked on the red clay earth under the harsh Australian sun. A young boy lying in the shade in one of the paintings stood up, looked at Sy and waved.

Sy looked around to see if anyone else had noticed. Had he imagined it? The boy waved again, ran right out of the painting, across the museum wall, and jumped into the next painting where a group of people were cooking at a camp fire. The minute he arrived, those inside sprang to life. Sy watched, mesmerized, as the little boy approached the adults and pointed out at Sy. He waved again, then ran out of that painting and jumped into a third, alerting the people there as well.

Sy waved back, as unobtrusively as possible.

The boy beckoned to him directly. Sy took the

tiniest step and hesitated, his senses alert. His class-mates had disappeared around a corner, leaving him alone in the room, which now seemed unnaturally silent and uncomfortably warm.

The boy gestured urgently, encouraging him to come closer. Sy moved slowly, inch by inch, with the boy beckoning at every step, until he was inches from the canvas, close enough for the boy to lean out, grab him roughly by the shoulders and pull him into the painting.

Sy looked around. Where was he? Could he really be inside the painting, or was he somewhere in the Australian outback hundreds of years ago? No one seemed surprised that an American teenager dressed in school uniform was standing among them. The men continued dancing while the women and children watched.

Sy stood there, uncertain, but somehow unafraid. The boy clasped Sy's hand with his small fingers and led him to the circle.

One of the men locked eyes with Sy.

"My uncle," the young boy said, his angelic face beaming with pride.

How cool—he understood the boy perfectly. His universal translator must be doing its job. Sy was grateful he could communicate. "I'm Sy," he said. "What's your name?"

"Aruma," the boy replied.

Sy smiled; because of his translator, he knew *aruma* also meant "happy."

"Why am I here, Aruma?" he asked.

Aruma patted his hand. "We have been waiting," he said.

A shadow blocked the sun. Sy found himself face to face with the man who'd been staring at him.

"You are now ready," said Aruma's uncle. "Follow me."

Aruma led Sy to the other side of the fire, where several women cleared a space for him. The oldest man he'd ever seen sat cross-legged; his dark face was creased with lines, his hair and beard white. His brown eyes were alert and seemed to be sending a message to Sy, one which Sy did not understand.

"Our respected elder," stated Aruma's uncle.

The elder nodded and indicated for Sy to sit next to him. Aruma sat by his side, patting his arm as if to reassure Sy that he was in good hands. With a wave of the elder's hand, the dancing and singing resumed.

Aruma's uncle reverently placed a clay cup on the ground before the old man. The elder put his beautiful wooden spear into the fire. When the tip glowed red, he lifted it out and touched the rim of the cup with the burning spearhead. Flames rose higher and higher. The fire hovered above the cup, spinning into a circle, then shot upward into the sky and flew to the east.

The elder quenched the spear's fire by digging into the dirt. A trickle of clear water dribbled out of the red clay earth, building in force until it was a delicate fountain. The elder held the cup under the gushing spray. When it was full and running over, the water shot upward, spinning into the sky, and the circle of water disappeared to the north.

The old man dug the spear again into the earth and, gathering up the loose dirt, sprinkled a handful into the cup. The soil shot out again, flew up and, spinning in a circle, disappeared to the south.

Air's next, thought Sy, and watched as the elder held up the cup and breathed into it. A mini-twister formed, soared into the sky and headed west.

The dancing was stilled and there was a silence. All eyes were on the elder and on Sy. He was aware of the heat, buzzing flies, birdsong, and the amazing energy he felt from sitting among people who seemed in harmony with all the forces of nature. The cup lay quiet at Sy's feet. He wondered what would happen next.

The elder broke the silence with his quiet, distinguished voice. "The Four Winds have been released and gone to rule over each corner of the world: north, south, east and west. Part of their spirit remains within this cup that sits in front of the boy." His aged hands rested for a moment on Sy's bare arm. "Drink from the cup and it shall guide you to gateways across all realms." The elder whispered into the cup and put it in Sy's trembling hands. "Drink."

It wasn't a request. Sy felt his stomach tighten in apprehension: the cup was full of a greenish liquid and it did not look appealing. He held the cup up to his lips to sip and hesitated; maybe the easiest way was to chug it.

It tasted like bark and mint, and wasn't that bad.

Sy felt his toes and fingers go numb. He seemed to be vibrating on the inside, but outwardly he was still.

The elder nodded his approval. "The power is now in you and no other," he said. He stood, and Sy rose with him. The leader placed his hands on Sy's shoulders, his grip surprisingly firm for such an old man.

Sy felt dizzy. It must be the heat, he thought. His vision blurred. He rubbed his eyes and heard his teacher say, "Sy, you're keeping everyone waiting."

He was back in the air-conditioned Guggenheim with his very unimpressed-looking teacher. How long had he been gone? "Sy!" his teacher said. "Let's go."

Sy hurried off to catch up with his class. As he rounded the corner, he looked back; the canvases were still, the figures frozen in time.

9

The Lunar Festival

Sy looked for Ryder as soon as he got to the Middle Realm; he wasn't in any of the regular places. "I.N.C.— Joshua Ryderson, Earth-tribe," he said.

Ryder's face appeared.

"Where are you?" Sy asked impatiently. "I need to tell you something!"

"It'll have to wait. I'm training my team and we'll probably be a while," said Ryder. "Tomorrow?" he offered.

"All right," said Sy, feeling a little rejected. He knew he was being a bit unfair, but Ryder was the only one he could really talk to.

"Sorry, Sy, but I've gotta go," Ryder said. "The festival is just around the corner, and I owe it to my team to be ready. You're cool, right? Later."

Ryder broke the connection.

* * *

Sy went straight around to Ryder's after school but, annoyingly, Samuel insisted they finish their homework before they could do anything. He made them bring their books into the kitchen and sat there drinking coffee and keeping up with Middle Realm news on his I.N.C. while they studied. After an hour, Ryder finally got Samuel to agree to let them get out for a bit. "We need a break. We'll just get some pizza and finish up when we get back," he promised.

Samuel looked skeptical, but let them go.

"Finally!" said Ryder, taking a huge bite of his pizza slice. "So what's so urgent it couldn't wait?"

Sy filled him in on everything that had transpired at the Guggenheim.

Ryder was quiet.

"So what do you think?" asked Sy.

"I'm not exactly sure." Ryder frowned. "Maybe you should ask Taurus."

Sy wasn't sure he was ready to face Taurus after their last encounter. He was about to say something to that effect when Samuel appeared on the I.N.C. "Time's up," he said.

Ryder hastily downed his soda. "Let's go," he said.

As they headed up Fourteenth Street, Sy nearly collided with two trolls. They were different from Nudd: tall and skinny with shaggy hair and long, skinny noses, and each had one large eye in the middle of its forehead that darted around, eagerly absorbing the sights of the street.

"That reminds me of those goblins I saw on that tour bus," said Sy.

"Sometimes I think there are more goblins in Manhattan than in the entire Middle Realm," said Ryder. "If you thought the city was crowded before, just wait. Goblins are major pranksters. I've got to give them credit, though; it's a much cooler Manhattan than most people get to see. Tourists cop the worse of it, though."

"Yeah . . . like those poor guys on the bus."

"Goblins love hassling tourists. They're in all the major cities across the Lower Realm, especially tourist hot spots." Ryder quickened his pace. "They've set up a huge holographic projection in the middle of Times Square—you know, above that ticket stand where people buy those half-price Broadway tickets—and they run a reality show called *GobCam* twenty-four seven: thousands of goblins laughing at tourists as they lose things and get lost. They'll do almost anything to get a laugh. They have surveillance throughout the city capturing every embarrassing tourist experience. They even keep score with a running tally, giving each goblin points if they directly caused the incident. You get bonus points if the event gets aired on GobCam." Ryder shook his head, smiling.

"What about trolls?" asked Sy, watching one stir

sugar into his take-out coffee with his long, skinny nose. "Do they mess with the tourists?"

"They're here to eat non-triber food. They're always walking through restaurants and helping themselves. They love leftovers and have the most disgusting table manners." Ryder screwed his face in distaste. "I don't like sharing my food," he said. "Triber cafes are safe zones for tribers in the Lower Realm. They're around, if you know where to look. You can mix with magical creatures and talk freely. It's great, because you can eat in peace."

Back at Ryder's, Sy didn't get a chance to talk any further about Aruma, or his missing brother, because Ryder was preoccupied with perfecting his training drill. This was his first challenge as a team leader, and even though he and Xanthia collaborated a lot, Sy knew he was fiercely competitive.

Later, getting ready for bed, Sy reflected on how much had happened to him recently. He burned with impatience to get started on finding Gabriel, but the festival was tomorrow night and he couldn't blame Ryder and everyone else for being so focused—it just didn't seem to be the right time to get into it. That didn't stop him from cringing, though, every time he remembered his "vision."

* * *

It was the month of Gemini, which belonged to Air-tribe. There would be no new arrivals or departures from Earth-tribe during the Gemini moon. Xanthia, Raf and Brady had arranged to meet Sy and Zak for a "what if" team briefing before the festival began, and Sy looked for them as soon as he arrived.

Xanthia was issuing last-minute instructions. She was very thorough; it was clear she wanted to make sure every base was covered. "And remember, if your forcefield doesn't work, then . . ."

Xanthia suddenly lost concentration. Sy followed her gaze to Ryder.

"Hey," Ryder greeted them. He gave his attention to Sy and Zak. "Are you guys ready?"

"We're nervous," said Zak.

"Isobel wants you," Raf said, nodding toward her as she approached, and smirking at her annoyed expression.

Isobel gave Ryder a dirty look. "You do realize this is not your team, don't you?" she snapped.

Ryder answered her with his most careless grin.

"Au revoir," she called to them, leading him away.

"Right," said Xanthia, tying back her long hair. "Are we ready?" She looked at them, one by one. "We're ready," she concluded.

Sy felt his stomach tighten and hoped he wouldn't let her down.

Buzzing with excitement, the team arrived at the big white central tent where they'd had their first initiation. No matter how many tribers entered, the space automatically expanded to accommodate them. The drapes were parted, and Sy could see all three Zodiac Council Earth leaders were already inside, smiling at everyone. Taurus, Sy knew, of course, but he was taken aback by Virgo—a stunning young woman with long blonde hair, and by Capricorn—a serious-looking goat with silver horns and a long white goatee.

"Welcome, Earth-tribers." Virgo beamed. "We are proud of each and every one of you, and hope you enjoy the festival. Team leaders, remember to look after your newest tribers. As always, unless you are competing, you must remain within the stadium until the festival is over."

Everyone cheered. Sy felt wound up and, looking around, saw he was not alone. The adrenalin in the room was palpable—like athletes before a major event. The tribers in front of Sy disappeared as they stepped into the glowing Earth-tribe circle. At last it was his turn. He took a step forward and shut his eyes tight.

Nothing happened.

He opened them, apologetic, expecting to see Taurus and the other tribers, but instead blinked in surprise. He was standing in a vast, circular stadium, much larger than Madison Square Gardens. It was daylight and, every so often, flashes of white light exploded across the violet Middle Realm sky. The stadium was divided into four main sections, one for each tribe.

The four clear tribal symbols, all intersecting, were engraved in the surface of the platform in the center of the stadium: the Twin Peaks of Legov in green for Earth-tribe; the Swirling Wind in white for Air-tribe; the Three Oceans of the Middle Realm in blue for Water-tribe and the red Four Flames of Bind-ush for Fire. Each team's symbol emitted light in their tribal color. Like the other tribers, Sy had been tele-ported directly to his team's symbol.

The seating swept back from each symbol. Between the designated tribal areas were seats for the creatures of the Middle Realm, including the Tribal-elite. Sy waved shyly at Samuel; knowing he was there was reassuring. Near Ryder's grandfather, gnomes and elves sat with goblins and fairies. They made a colorful sight.

Above the platform, the Zodiac Council hovered magnificently, more relaxed in midair than Sy was on solid ground. It was awe-inspiring, seeing them together: living representations of the zodiac symbols. Their presence was palpable as they watched the arriv-ing tribers with great pleasure and chattered amicably among themselves.

Sy turned to ask Zak what he thought, but stopped short. Zak wasn't wearing the jeans and shirt he'd had on a moment ago. Instead he wore protective body armor: silver metallic with green stripes down the arms and legs. There was an additional protec-tive layer that ran up the length of his spine and an armguard that reached his shoulders, as well as shin and knee guards. On the back of the suit was the green Earth-tribe symbol and "ZAK" in capital letters.

Sy looked down and saw that he too, along with every other triber, was decked out in a tribal competition suit—with his name emblazoned on his back.

Sy thought Air-tribe looked particularly cool, their faces painted white with a single red stripe down the center of their noses and eyes heavily outlined in black. Their suits were similar to Earth-tribe's, but all white with black-and-white hoods.

Ryder appeared up through the excited crowd. "This gear fits like a second skin and protects us in the challenges," he told Sy and Zak, who were still checking out each other's suits. "It's amazing—heat and cold resistant, waterproof and tear-proof. No matter what you do or what powers you come up against from other tribers during the challenge, your body's protected from serious injury. Selection is random, so everyone's dressed, just in case."

Sy looked around the stadium: all strangers, yet he felt connected to this new group to which he now belonged. He was a triber! He flew with his team to their seats in the green section.

The chatter died away and everyone's attention riveted on a tall, muscular man who magically appeared in the middle of the platform. His face was tattooed with all four tribal symbols. He wore a long red coat that fanned out behind him, a black fur hat and commanded immediate attention.

"The Ringmaster," whispered Ryder, who'd squeezed himself between Sy and Xanthia and was snacking on chocolate candy.

The Ringmaster's voice was deep and powerful. "Welcome tribers, mythical friends, Tribal-elite, Council members and honored guests," he roared, nodding respectfully to the Zodiac Council. "On behalf of our esteemed Council, we enter the month of Gemini."

He raised his muscular arms in the air. "Let the festival commence!" he boomed.

There was a roar as all over the stadium everyone cheered, craning their heads in anticipation of the entertainment.

"Look, it's the *Sphinxes*!" said Ryder, delighted.

Sy looked on in wonder as six giant black panthers with huge wings and massive paws took to the stage, the most beautiful fairies perched on their backs. The big cats were sleek, swooping over and under each other with a feline grace that belied their size.

The fairies were midair acrobats performing the most awesome display with the winged panthers as their nets; leaping from the panthers in multiple backflips to somersault through rings of fire and landing gracefully. The performance ended to a roar of applause. Accompanied by music and fireworks, the fairies perched daintily on their panthers and circled the stadium.

They vanished and the Ringmaster reappeared. A hush fell; the room became tense with anticipation. The Ringmaster materialized an impressive platinum metal staff and raised it in the air. He struck the platform forcefully, three times, the sound reverberating around the stadium. A metal circle rose from beneath his feet and started to spin at speed.

"Select," he commanded loudly.

Bright beams of red, blue, white and green light shot from the spinning circle. Sy froze as the green hit his chest and encased him in the colored light of his tribe.

"Bloody brilliant," said Zak, also encased.

"Here we go," said Brady quietly.

Xanthia's team was teleported to the platform to walk a lap around the stadium while their fellow tribers shouted their support and encouragement. Serious yet clearly energized, Xanthia introduced Sy and Zak to tribers from the other teams who had been selected. Everyone was friendly; there was an international feel as Sy was introduced to tribers from Denmark, Iceland, Russia, Sweden, Spain, Algeria, India, Morocco and Venezuela. There was a sense of camaraderie among the teams, even though they were competing. The only exceptions were two aloof Fire-tribe Level-7s, who also happened to be the tribers Sy most wanted to meet.

"I'm sure you recognize Dax Hunter and Lloyd Bellamy, or LB as the media call him," said Xanthia.

"They've won more individual challenges than anyone over the last five years and are our strongest competition. Watch out for them. They'll do anything to win."

"Dax is an awesome actor. I'm a big fan." Sy realized he sounded like a groupie, but he was unable to help himself.

"Lower Realm celebrity status means nothing here," said Xanthia sharply.

Sy couldn't help but watch the two actors with interest. Dax's blond crew cut and blue eyes were on countless magazine covers, and English LB, with his darker, longer hair and brown eyes, was the toast of both US and UK celebrity news. You didn't even have to be that much of a fan to know they were fitness freaks who shared a mansion in Beverly Hills. Sy had also read that they were close friends who surfed almost every day, were total players and had a reputation for partying.

Sy noticed how confidently they strutted around, creating a stir, especially with the girls who were vying for their attention. The other teams seemed a bit intimidated and moved aside for them.

They definitely had it in for Xanthia. Sy guessed success at such a young age meant that Dax and LB were now accustomed to and expected a privileged existence, with people bending over backward for them. Xanthia's rejection was a blow—some sort of hit to Dax's ego, he supposed.

They gave her a look of contempt as she moved past them and whispered something that caused their Fire team to erupt in laughter. When she turned defiantly, Dax stared her down. The entire group followed his lead, trying to intimidate her. Sy was impressed at how she pulled herself together and maintained her poise.

Xanthia looked away first. "He's just a sore loser," she said uncomfortably. "We need to keep focused and win this challenge." Her voice had a steely edge.

The lap complete, the Ringmaster spoke formally to the teams. "Today's challenge is a race," he instructed.

Sy was fascinated to see himself in a projected image in front of the Earth-tribe section of the stadium. The other tribes were provided with the same close-up view of their team members.

Brady noticed him looking. "They're holographic projections, so everybody can watch us compete. Kinda like being on TV, I guess. Challenges usually happen outside the stadium," he explained.

"Bloody brilliant," said Zak, and Raf laughed.

A scroll appeared in each team leader's hands. Xanthia opened it and read:

Untouched and divine,
Each one you must find.
All the days of the week

Correspond to the number you seek.
One, the highest in the land,
While another thrives on the sand.
An erupting volcano caused havoc and fear.
The statue stands proud, his arms spread far
    and near.
Thunderous water cascades in a sheet,
In a place where wild animals graze in the heat.
In this place, eroded rock has formed a steep hole.
For a spectacular show, try the North Pole.

The team exchanged blank looks. Xanthia read it again. Dax's team took off with a roar of support from Fire-tribe. "How did they work it out so quickly?" she asked in frustration.

They reviewed the clues again.

"Well, the highest in the land—that could be Mount Everest, couldn't it?" Zak suggested cautiously.

"And I think another could be the Redeemer statue in the harbor of Rio de Janeiro," said Raf.

"Good, what do they have in common?" asked Xanthia, thinking hard.

"Everest and the harbor of Rio de Janeiro are both natural wonders of the world in the Lower Realm," said Brady in his quiet way. "Seven wonders, seven days of the week, maybe?"

"That's it!" said Xanthia excitedly.

"The Great Barrier Reef in Australia is another,"

suggested Sy, breaking into a grin when Xanthia beamed at him.

They quickly worked out the Grand Canyon in Arizona, Victoria Falls in Africa and the Paricutin Volcano in Mexico. The crowd roared again, distracting them, and Water and Air took to the sky. "What's the last one?" asked Raf urgently.

They re-read the clues, but no one knew what it was.

Raf was frowning. "What's near the North Pole?"

"Some sort of famous glacier?" suggested Zak.

"We'll split into two groups and get to the places we know," instructed Xanthia. "I'll check the I.N.C. en route and let you know the last wonder."

To the relief of Ryder and the other Earth-tribers, Xanthia's team finally left the stadium. Zak, Raf and Brady took off and Sy was paired with Xanthia.

Sy tried to ignore how awesome his team leader looked in her body armor. He hoped he wouldn't let her down. She was so smart and cool under pressure, and he knew how much it meant to her to win.

"For getting places fast, I always use Directories, because they know the hidden portals," Xanthia told him. She whistled through two fingers. A silver hexahedron cube appeared and skidded to a hovering halt. It had twelve edges, and inside was a floating head with an angular, chiseled face that looked computer generated.

"Directory 231 at your service," it said.

"Rio de Janeiro, Brazil, Lower Realm," she instructed.

The hexahedron spun to reveal a tribal symbol on one of its sides. Xanthia placed her palm on the symbol.

"Verified, access granted."

The Directory increased in size, and two side panels dissolved, revealing seats. Xanthia jumped in, followed by an amazed Sy.

A mind-blowingly short time later, they saw the glistening bay of Rio de Janeiro with the statute of the Redeemer overlooking the Metropolis, surrounded by the city and the mountains. In the water they saw the four tribal symbols.

As they flew to the symbols, Sy gestured to Xanthia; Air-tribe were racing in from another direction. The Earth-tribers sped up, but it was going to be close.

Xanthia and Sy were hit with a strong blast of icy wind that pushed them backward and rocked them from side to side.

"Rock wall!" shouted Xanthia, and it was as if she was gathering and pushing at the air, but in her hands it turned to clay and rock, spreading and thickening, forming a wall between them and the blast.

At a loss at how else to help, Sy made a forcefield to protect her while she worked. Sheltered by the wall, they sped to the water.

Air-tribe's team leader raised his arms and, instantly, gray storm clouds appeared and bolts of white lightning blasted down, blocking the path between the Earth-tribers and the tribal symbols.

Before Xanthia and Sy could recover, Air team registered its arrival on their symbol. The wind and lightning disappeared, and the victors left the scene, laughing and chatting.

Xanthia let the rock wall dissolve and flew with Sy over the harbor's shining water. She placed her palm on the Earth-tribe symbol.

"Congratulations on finding this wonder. You're the last team to arrive."

Xanthia's face said it all.

The Directory hovered, waiting while Sy used the I.N.C. to research their next destination and Xanthia contacted the others. The news was thrilling. Earth-tribe had been first in Australia and second in Africa. The other three were in a Directory on the way to the Paricutin Volcano in Mexico.

* * *

Ryder watched the holographic action, completely riveted. He'd gotten over his disappointment at not competing himself and was hoarse from cheering on Xanthia and her team. He checked how the other tribes were doing and his heart sank; Dax and LB had reached Mount Everest first and stayed behind, sending the rest of their team on while they planned an ambush. He knew they wanted to win this challenge, no matter what, and that if they won, they'd make sure Xanthia was taught a lesson in humility. Ryder's mouth was set in a hard line. He really couldn't stand those two.

The Water team was well on its way to the mountain. Fire-tribe had a major rivalry with the Water-tribers, and Ryder could see Dax and LB were itching to mess with them. Using their Fire powers to keep themselves from freezing, they lay quietly, hidden in the snow, waiting . . .

Water-tribe appeared, talking excitedly. They were about to register their arrival on their symbol when the two Level-7s sprang out of the snow. Dax shot a fireball and Water-tribe's team leader warded it off, extinguishing the flame with a streaming blast of water from his palm. LB opened his mouth and breathed fire. He controlled the flames with his voice, instructing them to circle the Water team while Dax kept them busy, bombarding them with fireballs; within minutes the Water-tribers were imprisoned inside LB's encircling wall of flame.

Dax raised his hands and drew down enormous energy to create a fire-rock in midair. The Water-tribers tried helplessly to extinguish the flames, but they were no match for Dax and LB. The wall of fire became a fiery prison with intense heat now above and below. Water powers and body armor protected the team against the flames and heat, but could not help with their incarceration. The Water-tribers were clearly going to be stuck on the top of Mount Everest for a while, ruling out their chances of winning.

Ryder's disappointed groan was drowned out by enormous cheers from the Fire-tribers, who hero-worshipped Dax and LB. An ambush from the shadows may not have been considered good sportsmanship, but was well within the rules . . . only light-speed tele-porting by Level-7s was forbidden, to keep things fair.

* * *

Raf I.N.C.'d Xanthia from Mount Everest and gave them the update. Xanthia shook her head at how low Dax and LB were. "But it improves our odds of winning," she said.

Sy thought he might have figured out the last wonder. "I reckon it's the Northern Lights," he said. Xanthia had ignited his own competitive spirit and now he really wanted to win. Sy used the I.N.C. to pull up an image of the Northern Lights, while Xanthia quickly arranged to meet the rest of the team there.

"The Northern Lights are found predominantly at night in the highest parts of the Northern Hemi-sphere," Sy said, scanning the text on the screen. "One of the best places to see the spectacular light show, also known as the Aurora Borealis, is in Norway," he read out.

On Xanthia's urgent instruction, the hexahedron sped to Norway. Sy kept the image of the lights on the I.N.C. A short time later they saw another hexahedron behind them, slowly gaining speed. "It's Fire-tribe," Xanthia said, frowning. "Step on it," she instructed their Directory urgently.

Sy looked on anxiously as Fire-tribe caught up. Tense moments later, Dax and LB emerged from the moving hexahedron and flew closer. Grinning spitefully, they created a giant fireball and threw it right at them.

The Directory swerved dangerously. Sy's head butted against the I.N.C. image and he felt himself hurtling forward. Instinctively, he grabbed Xanthia's arm. Seconds later they found themselves witnessing the Northern Lights, somewhere near the North Pole . . .

"What happened?" asked Xanthia, clearly shocked.

Sy was equally surprised but thought he could guess what had happened. He told her about being transported inside the paintings at his school excursion.

"Awesome," she said, looking around. "I think we've arrived exactly where we need to be . . ."

White and blue swirling flashes crossed the dark gray sky. With a thrill, they spotted the four tribal symbols.

Dax and LB's Directory arrived and sped toward them.

"Hurry!" shouted Xanthia.

Sy slammed his palm on the Earth symbol.

"Congratulations," a voice said. "You are the first tribe to arrive. Your team has now successfully completed its task and wins this month's challenge."

They looked at each other in amazed excitement. The last thing they glimpsed before being teleported back to the stadium was the shocked and furious faces of the Fire team.

* * *

Back at basecamp they were treated like heroes. A crowd had gathered around them and Xanthia was positively glowing. Sy was so happy for her; she'd put in the effort, worked hard and he was thrilled to see her enjoying the well-deserved rewards. The Fire-tribers had only missed out on winning by seconds. Her success just motivated her to continue to strive for excellence.

"How did you do it?" Nudd asked Sy.

"I'm not exactly sure," he replied.

"I am so happy for you!" Isobel told Xanthia, hugging her.

Raf and Brady were hoisted in the air on the shoulders of jubilant tribers, while Zak kept shouting, "Bloody brilliant!"

Ryder pushed through the crowd, impatient to congratulate Xanthia and the rest of the team. When he reached them, he pulled up and stood still, staring at Xanthia. She was back in her regular clothes and her legs looked endless in her tight jeans. She looked so happy, so unbelievably . . . hot.

She smiled at him. "Ryder!" she said, as if he were just who she wanted to see.

He took a step toward her and pulled her close for a hug but, instead of that, swept up in the moment and even though they could be seen by what seemed like the entire tribe, he kissed her.

Sy felt strange watching them. Ryder and Xanthia seemed completely oblivious to the appreciative wolf whistles—and Isobel's look of dismay.

10

Partying in Malibu

It felt great to be part of a winning team. Everyone was talking about how Sy and Xanthia had just beaten Dax and LB to the Northern Lights. Sy felt like he'd won the World Series.

Raf I.N.C.'d him. "Things are getting heavy," he said.

"Why?" said Sy.

"Xanthia has completely blown Ryder off."

"She's a very private person," Raf said. "Isobel is also keeping a low profile. I'm trying to smooth things over. There's major tension between those three."

Sy was obviously a lot less experienced with girls, but where Xanthia was concerned, he could completely understand Ryder's attraction. Just thinking about her in that way made him feel disloyal, even though it was obvious she was completely out of his league. He decided to put his friends out of his mind and concentrate on his upcoming LA trip.

Trent had been offered a friend's vacation house in Malibu for the weekend. Unfortunately for her, Rebecca had work commitments, and much to Sy's delight, Trent had suggested a boys' surf trip. His dad had been so busy promoting his movie, and Sy had been so wrapped up in the Middle Realm, he was looking forward to them hanging out together.

They caught the early morning flight out of JFK to LAX and, with the time difference, made it out to Malibu before lunch. They spent the rest of the day at the beach, stopping only to eat between surf sessions. Sy shared his dad's passion for the environment and especially the ocean. At sunset, they walked back to their rental car, both exhausted and exhilarated.

"Sy, your surfing has improved enormously," Trent told him.

Sy was thrilled. "You think?"

"Your confidence has gone to the next level," Trent observed, drying his hair with a towel. "You took on waves you never would have dared to before. I liked watching you."

Sy was touched by his dad's feedback. His confidence *had* improved since becoming a triber.

A couple of ATVs came rocketing down the beach toward them. Sy could hardly believe his eyes: the drivers were Dax and LB! They exchanged pleasantries, pretending they knew Sy through a mutual school friend. LB charmed Trent into bringing Sy to check out their place on the beach. "It's just up there." He pointed the glamorous house out to Trent, and to Sy's amazement, his dad agreed.

Their boards safely stowed on the board-racks, LB offered Sy his 450cc ATV and jumped on the back with Dax. Trent let Sy drive, and he followed Dax cautiously, feeling surreal and a little guilty. But it was so cool to be riding the ATV in the company of two major celebs. Maybe Dax and LB weren't so bad? And how awesome was it that they—*the* Dax and LB!—were interested in *him*!

Their pad on the beach was sick, with the most incredible views. They had a large staff—who were all busy catering for a huge party. Sy saw MTV cribs arrive, and gorgeous girls everywhere, in the pool and just hanging out. He was blown away, elated to be there. Celebrities were turning up every minute: famous models, rappers and movie stars. Trent even knew a few of the producers from his Wall Street days and was soon deep in conversation, leaving Sy free to take it all in.

Dax and LB were very attentive, introducing Sy as a good friend. This gave him automatic status, especially when the twins Chloe and Emile latched onto him. Sixteen-year-old models from France, they spoke very little English, but thanks to his translator, he understood them perfectly . . . if only he could think of something to say.

Sy couldn't find Trent anywhere, and when Dax and LB asked him to join them privately, he felt a tremor of trepidation. What a relief it was when they just congratulated him warmly on his team's great win at the lunar festival and asked lots of questions about how he'd been teleported to the Northern Lights. Sy told them everything he knew.

On the flight home, Sy and his dad went over the details, Trent teasing Sy that he was star struck. The only time Sy's enthusiasm waned was when he imagined Xanthia and Ryder's reaction.

* * *

A few days later, he had a chance to find out what that reaction might be. He caught up with Samuel and Ryder at the warehouse, and they sat in the kitchen, reliving the highlights of the festival.

"You always remember your first challenge," Samuel told Sy affectionately.

"It would be great if Sy could replay the festival win," said Ryder, smiling at his grandfather.

"I can help you travel through your own mind to view every happy and joyous moment from your past," Samuel explained. "You'll be able to view everything you've experienced in a flash. Ryder loves it, but it's okay if you don't want to—it's not for everyone."

"It's a real rush," said Ryder.

Sy's pulse quickened with excitement. Maybe he would see his brother?

"Your body is an incredible machine," said Samuel. "The brain stores the data, and your memories are linked with an emotional response. The same chemical is released in your body when you relive the event."

"For sure, I'll give it a go," said Sy.

"It's quite safe and private," replied Samuel. "Your memories are your own unless you choose to share them. Close your eyes."

"I'm going to I.N.C. Xanthia again," Ryder said, leaving them to it.

Samuel touched Sy in the center of his forehead, above his eyes. Instantly, incredible imagery flashed before him: baby memories, birthdays, surfing, family vacations, sounds, smells . . . every detail. But there was no sign of Gabriel, and through his great joy he felt a stab of disappointment. Nevertheless, when it was over, he was recharged and felt absolutely appreciative of his life. After a few moments he said, "That was intense . . . thank you."

"My pleasure. Though, I must say, I am still quite interested in how you were teleported to the lights," Samuel said.

"So are Dax and LB," said Ryder, leaping down the stairs two at a time, his expression furious. "They've made an official request for Earth team to be disqualified."

"Why?" asked Sy with a sinking sensation in his stomach.

"Raf just told me they've lodged a protest, saying you won unfairly by teleporting to the Northern Lights when they aren't allowed to use their Level-7 power of travel at light speed. Their council leader, Leo, is in discussion with Taurus."

"Tell me what you know about how you teleported," Samuel said to Sy.

Sy filled him in on his encounter at the Guggenheim. Samuel was quiet for a few moments. "A myth about the Four Winds exists," he said thoughtfully. "I'll find out more . . ."

Sy's heart sank. He couldn't bring himself to tell them about hanging out with Dax and LB in Malibu. What if he'd cost his team a precious win by opening his big mouth? Ryder was clearly angry. Sy convinced himself that it would be better to wait for a more appropriate time—and maybe the Zodiac Council would rule in Earth-tribe's favor and no one would ever have to know he'd told Dax and LB too much about his power.

On his way home, Sy made a quick stop in Times Square. As he crossed Broadway and Forty-Second Street, he noticed a holographic billboard he'd never seen before, right next to the NASDAQ sign. He stared in surprise: there was Xanthia, being interviewed about her recent lunar festival win! There was no mention of disqualification. Maybe the whole thing was already forgotten.

There were other bulletins with all sorts of Middle Realm news. Ryder had told him there were numerous Middle Realm noticeboards in the Lower Realm, invisible to everyone but tribers. You just had to know where to look. His sense of contentment and high energy continued for the rest of the day, and he breezed through his homework.

That night he lay in bed thinking about his friends. The gossip at basecamp was that everyone had been expecting Ryder and Xanthia to hook up for ages. It seemed inevitable they would be together. He supposed he should be happy for Ryder. He knew there was no way he would ever rate with Xanthia as an option; he was too young, for a start. He wasn't even sure how he'd handle it if someone like Xanthia *did* like him. He'd barely been able to talk to Chloe and Emile at Dax's party. Most of his friends used Facebook, rather than talk to girls directly. It was a much easier option.

He arrived at basecamp that evening and headed straight for the Lounge. It was virtually empty. Without the usual laughter, noise and teenage antics, the room had a slightly melancholy feel. The walls were gray and the music subdued.

He ordered a soda and sank into one of the armchairs. Whenever he was alone, he thought about

Gabriel. Where was he right now? Did he know about Sy? What did the golden device *mean* . . .?

He heard a familiar voice and swiveled around to see Xanthia. She had her back to him and was talking on the I.N.C. to a girl he recognized from the festival: tall, Nordic-looking Dana who was a team leader from Air-tribe.

"It's sooo obvious what it means," drawled Dana.

"I don't know," Xanthia argued. "He got caught up in the moment . . . all that excitement and getting one up on Dax and LB."

Her friend sighed. "Xanthia, why can't you admit you like him? Your entire tribe knows he's into you. He's totally hot! Just go for it!"

Sy didn't know what to do. He didn't want to be listening to her conversation, but if he moved, he'd give himself away. He sank lower into his chair.

Dana narrowed her eyes. "Are you worried about Isobel?"

"I really need to focus on my training," Xanthia said, clearly uncomfortable. "Thanks, Dana, but I've gotta go," she finished brusquely and signed out.

Xanthia's mouth dropped open in horror when she discovered him sitting there, fervently wishing he were anywhere else. "Sy!" she exclaimed. "What are you doing?"

Sy was mortified. He mumbled a response, but at that exact moment, Ryder turned up. His eyes scanned the room and locked on Xanthia's. For a split second, the three of them froze. Ryder was the first to recover. He headed over.

"Hey guys," he said, nodding to Sy but looking pointedly at Xanthia with an unspoken question in his eyes.

"Hi," she said. "I was just leaving."

Ryder looked hurt. "Where are you going?"

She nearly knocked over Sy's soda in her haste to get away. "I'm meeting someone," she said, vaguely waving back at them. "See you both later."

Ryder stared after her, disappointment etched on his face. Sy thought about telling him what he'd overheard, but didn't know how. Perhaps it was better not to interfere.

"Samuel found out more about the Four Winds, and he's coming here to see you," Ryder told him, forcing himself to get it together. "He's meeting us in my tent. Let's go."

The Lounge was filling up, and the atmosphere was more upbeat. They made their way through the crowd. Before Sy's eyes, the walls transformed to a deep maroon, the lighting dimmed and glowing lamps appeared on the tables. An R&B band materialized on the stage, already playing.

Samuel was waiting at Ryder's tent. He smiled warmly, and Sy sat down eagerly.

"I believe your experience in the Guggenheim

is connected to a legend, very mysterious and very old," said Samuel. "The story goes that there was a young man who longed to be admired. He had powerful magic and used it to control the elements. As his power increased, he became feared, arrogant and vain, no longer showing his gratitude to the elements that served him. It became his desire to rule the sun, preside over the moon and control the weather.

"Eventually, the sun called a meeting with the moon and it was agreed that the Four Winds would teach this man a lesson in humility.

"The north wind blew him to the North Pole and left him on the top of the highest mountain, where he almost froze. The southern wind captured him and blew him to the southernmost point of the world in Antarctica. He was encased in snow and barely alive when the east wind blew him to the easternmost point on the planet, Caroline Island, Kiribati. The wind blew into his ears until they ached and he was screaming. Finally, when he was weakened and dying, the west wind blew him to Alaska before returning him home, where it breathed life back into him.

"He understood then that he was not above the elements after all. In fact, the opposite was true. He owed his life to them and made it his life's purpose to demonstrate his respect to the sun and the moon. He dedicated his life to honor the winds that had taught him such a valuable lesson and had, in their mercy, spared his life.

"On the last day of his life on earth, he lay quietly, holding the hands of his wife, surrounded by his six sons and seven daughters. A great breeze blew into the modest hut where they lived, raising the dust and sending the lizards scurrying. The Winds had come to offer their tribute to the man they now considered a friend. They whispered the power into his ear, and he shared it with his wife—with instructions to guard the secret of how to pass it on."

"What was the power?" asked Sy.

"The ability to journey to every corner of the world where the Four Winds blew," said Samuel.

"How?"

"By jumping into a cave painting, drawing, or representation of the place they wanted to visit."

Samuel appraised him carefully. "Sy, I believe you ingested the power when you drank from the clay cup. The Four Winds are now a part of you. You are now able to travel through paintings, photos, images—anything that can act as your portal."

Ryder exhaled loudly, completely impressed. "Awesome! So, Sy can just jump into a photo and be wherever the picture was taken?" he asked.

"Exactly." Samuel beamed. "And if I am correct, you will also be able to travel through time."

Ryder was even more impressed. "Even Level-7s can't do that!"

"But why me?" said Sy.

Samuel looked thoughtful but had no more knowledge to share. "All I can advise is: use your power wisely and with discretion," he said. "Power always has its consequences."

"I.N.C. me when you're done with training," said Ryder. "And we can grab something to eat."

* * *

Sy headed toward the Level-1 tent.

"How's Isobel?" Zak asked him.

"I haven't seen her," said Sy. "Any news on whether we're going to be disqualified?"

"Not yet," said Zak. "Dax and LB are gits."

Sy nodded, feeling awful.

Taurus arrived. "Hello, everyone," he said, smiling. "Welcome to DNA Enhancements. As tribers, you have been granted many new abilities, including increased brain functionality—giving you access to areas in your brain that non-tribers rarely tap into."

After DNA Enhancements, they practiced the Shadow Concealment Power. Sy really struggled. For all his new-found confidence, he just couldn't overcome his claustrophobia. The idea that he would deliberately put himself in a confined space was not natural to him. He was making a huge effort to keep his fears in check, but still felt frustrated and embarrassed that he couldn't control his phobia. He couldn't wait for the session to be over so he could meet Ryder in the Lounge.

They sat at an empty table near the back so they could talk freely. "Burger and fries," Sy requested. "And an orange juice, please." A delicious-smelling burger appeared with a side order of golden frenchfries. The juice was freshly squeezed and frothy at the top.

"I'll have a stack of pancakes with pecan icecream. Oh, and a banana shake," said Ryder. "We need to test out your time-travel power." He drowned his pancakes in maple syrup. "Xanthia was teleported with you, so you can obviously bring a guest." He raised an eyebrow suggestively.

Sy tried to eat, but after a few fries he realized that he wasn't very hungry—too excited. Ryder had no such problem, apparently, the way he was wolfing his pancakes down.

"I don't even know exactly how to do it myself yet," Sy ventured.

"No time like the present, then." Ryder finished his shake and stood up impatiently. "You eating those fries?"

Sy shook his head.

Ryder grabbed a handful. "Well, there's no point wasting them!"

As they left the Lounge they almost collided with Zak and Isobel, walking in. There was a moment of tense silence.

"Hey," said Ryder.

"Hi," answered Zak, looking uncomfortable.

Isobel smiled at Sy, but would not meet Ryder's gaze.

"See you round," said Ryder awkwardly, and ushered Sy out quickly.

11

The Laboratory

As always, Sy felt strange coming from the sunshine and light of the Middle Realm to night-time in the Lower Realm. Ryder didn't say anything about their uncomfortable encounter with Isobel. Following his cue, Sy didn't bring it up either.

They snuck into the townhouse and quietly made their way to Trent's study. The room smelled of leather and polish. On his dad's desk were photographs in silver frames. Treasured moments from Sy's life from babyhood to teenager were recorded, frozen in time. What had Gabriel looked like as a baby? It was as if he had never existed . . .

Ryder checked out the photos as if he were examining travel brochures to see where to go on vacation. He stopped at a large photo in a beautiful Tiffany frame that showed a young Trent and Rebecca on their wedding day. They were in Italy and the shot was taken on one of Venice's beautiful bridges. With an intricately laced wrought-iron railing, it arched gracefully over the green water and joined the narrow lanes that were separated by the famous canals.

"Pizza in Venice?" Ryder suggested.

"I can't go in there. That's my parent's wedding day!"

"So? Italy is awesome."

"I don't even know exactly how to do it," argued Sy.

"Try," said Ryder, grabbing hold of his arm and pushing him toward the photograph.

Sy stared at the photo and back at Ryder, expectant, but nothing happened. "What am I meant to do?" he asked.

"Concentrate."

Sy concentrated, imagining his parents in Venice, but still nothing happened.

"What did you do on the challenge?" asked Ryder.

Sy thought back. For the Northern Lights, he'd made actual physical contact with the image. At the Guggenheim, he'd been dragged in. "Hold on," he said, grabbed Ryder by the arm, and dived in, head-first, hoping for the best.

Within the blink of an eye they were on the bridge among a small group of tourists watching the young couple on their wedding day in the still, warm afternoon. Sy cringed at the thought of explaining what he was doing there, but realized that they wouldn't know who he was.

It was a weird thought.

In any case, his parents were somewhat distracted. The wedding photographer was gesturing to them in a mixture of English and Italian. He expressed his delight when Trent finally got what he was on about and passionately embraced his new bride. "Bravo!" said the photographer, smiling. The few bystanders clapped appreciatively.

"Gross!" Sy turned away. "I wish you'd picked a different photo," he said irritably.

Ryder led him away from his parents. "Come on, let's head this way."

They walked down a few narrow lanes and found themselves at the famous Piazza St Marco. The sun was setting over the Grand Canal, and hundreds of pigeons walked among the tourists, eagerly pecking at crumbs. Ryder changed some money via the I.N.C., and they wandered into a shop to buy gelato and chocolate biscotti. They strolled for a while along the canals and checked it all out.

"I guess we'd better head back to the present," said Ryder.

"We don't really know how to get back," said Sy, feeling a little worried.

"I think the way we came in," Ryder said as they retraced their steps through the Piazza to the bridge.

Sy's parents were no longer there.

"There should be some gateway back at the exact

place where we arrived, shouldn't there?" said Ryder. "I'd say it was right here!"

They stood on the bridge, but nothing happened.

Sy had an idea. "I.N.C.—image of my house, East Seventy-Ninth Street, Manhattan," he said. The picture of his street appeared. Sy grabbed Ryder's arm, and in an instant they were outside his townhouse.

"That was sick!" Ryder enthused. Sy agreed, and couldn't wait to try it again. They looked around. "What the . . .?" said Ryder.

Sy's street was not how they'd left it—there were old-fashioned cars and lots of people in the street wearing strange clothes.

"I think we've landed in the wrong century!" said Sy, feeling panicked. "It must be when the townhouse was first built or something."

"Try the I.N.C. image again," said Ryder nervously. "But you'd better specify the date."

"It better work here," said Sy.

To their great relief, the I.N.C. didn't seem to care what century it was, and they were soon safely back in the right place and time.

"Phew," said Sy. "Don't forget to tell your grandfather you're invited for dinner tomorrow evening," he said to Ryder before the sixty-second warning flashed and he woke up in his bed.

* * *

Ryder met him at his school the next afternoon so they could walk home to the brownstone together. It was humid and windy. Gray clouds hovered ominously over the city. The streets were busy as people hailed cabs and scurried into the subway to avoid what looked like an approaching storm.

"I hope we make it home before the rain," remarked Sy, looking up.

"The Council voted to retract Earth-tribe's win," said Ryder as soon as they were out of earshot of Sy's school buddies. "Xanthia will be furious."

Before Sy could respond to this terrible news, the two of them were grabbed from behind.

"Hey!" shouted Ryder.

The two stone gargoyles from down the street had come to life and lifted them into the air. They had powerful, muscular bodies with large webbed wings, and in their cruel faces their blank stone eyes were devoid of expression. Through a haze of shock, Sy saw razor-sharp teeth inside their wide mouths. Their freakishly human fingers gripped him painfully as they flew. He called out to Ryder, but his mouth filled with a disgusting-tasting substance that hardened like cement. Ryder seemed to be experiencing the same thing. His turquoise eyes widened in horror. Their mouths had been sealed shut, and struggling to breathe through their noses, neither could make a sound.

Sy wondered wildly whether he and Ryder were

being turned into gargoyles . . . he felt completely out of it: freezing, petrified, and he could barely breathe. He felt sick. Ryder started hyperventilating. Sy's eyes rolled and he —

* * *

Sy woke. "Ryder?"

"I'm here," Ryder answered.

Sy exhaled in relief. As his eyes adjusted to the semi-darkness, he made out that they were in a small room. It smelled musty. A single dull globe hung from a wire in the ceiling, casting eerie shadows on the walls and floor.

"Are you okay?" Ryder asked.

Sy wasn't sure how to answer. His head was throbbing and his throat was so parched he could barely swallow, but at least the cement had disappeared. "Where are we?" he asked, anxiously looking around.

"Beats me." Ryder sounded worried. "The I.N.C. isn't working. I tried to telepathically contact Raf or Xanthia but—nothing, just silence." Sy was in danger, Ryder thought. He'd promised Samuel he'd look out for him; it was imperative he keep a cool head . . .

Sy pressed his ear against the door, trying to hear what was on the other side. "Should we check it out?" he whispered.

Ryder wasn't keen. "What about the gargoyles?"

"But there's no other way out!" Sy looked

desperately around the small room, trying to suppress his rising panic. "I'm getting out of here." He tried the door and looked at Ryder in horror. "It's locked," he whispered.

"I have an idea." Ryder stood in front of the locked door and pulled Sy to his side. Sy saw their shadows on the floor before feeling himself suddenly squeezed into a small dark space. Just before he exploded into full-blown panic, he was on the other side of the door, Ryder beside him. He looked at Ryder, suddenly understanding. Ryder had just hidden them in his shadow and used it to slip under the door.

There was no sign of the gargoyles. They crept out and pressed their backs firmly against the wall, moving silently, their senses on full alert. They were in some kind of warehouse laboratory: all white, glass and stainless steel. There was a lot of high-tech futuristic machinery. Inching closer, they were shocked and disturbed to see a row of small incubators. Tiny infants lay on their backs inside them. Why were they here and not in a hospital? Seeing the infants there, helplessly trapped with tubes connected to their little heads made them feel very uncomfortable. An inky substance was being fed through the tubes.

They looked for a way out, but the warehouse was huge. Where the hell were they? Larger incubators were stacked in racks from floor to ceiling. The first few were empty, but the next revealed sleeping children, teenagers and adult humans. There were rows and rows of them lining the walls of the warehouse. The people inside each had a tube attached to their forehead that seemed to be pumping in black liquid.

What was going on?

A piercing wail penetrated the unnatural silence.

"What the hell is that?" hissed Sy.

"It came from over there," whispered Ryder, pointing to a door. They inched their way over and cautiously opened it, revealing a staircase that led to a basement. It was cold and dark and smelled like mold. The shrieking made their hair stand on end. "What is this place?" repeated Ryder.

"Someone's coming!" warned Sy.

They had no choice but to creep down the stairs and shut the door behind them.

A narrow corridor with many doors set into its walls led away into the darkness. All around was the sound of muffled crying and sobbing. One of the doors had a glass window. "I think the screaming came from in here," said Ryder. They peered through the glass and saw people shuffling around in white smocks. One guy was rocking back and forth on all fours, laughing hysterically; another was sobbing while licking the white linoleum floor.

"It's some kind of nut-house," whispered Ryder.

A mutilated face lunged out of the gloom and pressed right up against the glass. Sy jumped back in horror and stifled a scream. The creature had only half a face: one side with an eye, half a nose and half a mouth, but the other was meaty, raw flesh.

It was too much. They turned and bolted back up the stairs, no longer caring about what was coming, desperate to find a way out of the nightmare. Racing out, Ryder tripped and went flying, smashing into a stack of incubators. There was a loud, creaking noise and a moment of tense silence as the topmost one swayed dangerously. It fell with a *crash*! Glass smashed everywhere and Ryder cursed loudly, clutching at his knee. A blaring alarm pierced the air.

"Are you okay?" Sy asked.

But Ryder was no longer worried about his knee, or the alarm . . . he was staring at the girl on the floor who had fallen out of an incubator. It was Xanthia, lying motionless, her normally gorgeous blue eyes staring at them unseeing, a gluey black liquid seeping out of her mouth. Sy felt the blood drain from his face. They both knelt by her side.

"Xanthia!" Ryder said. He tried to lift her up, but almost dropped her. "That's not Xanthia," he said. "It can't be. That thing isn't human."

"R . . . R . . . Ryder . . . what's going on?" They heard footsteps and angry voices, even closer now. There was nowhere to hide. "I.N.C.—Central Park image," said Sy urgently.

Nothing happened.

"*Try again*!" Ryder shouted.

"I.N.C.—picture of Central Park, New York," Sy repeated in desperation.

No response.

A moment later they were confronted by five dark elves, their fluorescent eyes shining with fury.

"Forcefield!" screamed Ryder. The forcefield appeared but the elves threw black dust at them that dissolved it and dusted their faces, blinding them. Sy could hardly breathe. The elves seized him roughly. Sy jerked his body in an effort to break free. Ryder was also struggling, but the elves only held them tighter, cruelly twisting their arms behind their backs until they both cried out from the pain.

They were dragged a short way. Sy heard a door open, more screaming, and a nasty smell assailed his nostrils. They were being taken back into the basement! Fear, more intense than he had ever experienced, washed over him in great waves, causing his body to shake. His breathing was loud and labored. Thrown to the floor, he felt Ryder tossed down next to him. A door slammed.

It was quiet. Sy rubbed his stinging eyes and tried to control his breathing. "What are we going to do?" he whispered urgently.

When Ryder's vision cleared, he saw they were in a small room with the same white linoleum floor and walls he'd seen earlier. And they weren't alone: a man lay on the floor in the corner of the room, his knees clasped against his chest, rocking silently.

Well-built, in his early twenties with cropped dark hair and long silver chains around his neck, the stranger struck Ryder as somehow familiar.

"I —" Ryder gulped.

The man stared at them, rocked harder and burst into hysterical laughter. He faced the corner and they had not yet seen his face.

"Who are you?" Ryder managed.

"Who am I?" It was as if this question greatly amused him. "*Who am I* . . . Yes, who am I?" He kept repeating it over and over, laughing all the while.

Ryder turned away. "What are we going to do, Sy?"

"Excuse me —" The guy in the corner had stopped rocking, sat up, turned around and was leaning against the wall as if exhausted. "Does anyone know I'm gone?" he said. "Three number one albums, millions of fans around the world, and no one is looking for me?" A tear rolled down his cheek. "How is that possible?" He straightened. "They mustn't know."

"You're Mac Q!" Ryder said. "One of the biggest R&B stars on the planet!"

"Finally!" said Mac Q, sounding relieved.

"Oh wow," said Sy. "I've got all of your tracks on my iPod."

"Me too," said Ryder. "But what are you doing *here*?"

"Beats me." Mac Q shrugged, wearily. "One minute I'm on the way to lunch in the back of my limo, and the next I'm in some kind of laboratory incubator being subjected to all kinds of tests, like a regular lab rat."

"But I just saw you on the Internet—the other day—at the MTV awards," said Ryder.

"It wasn't me." Mac Q slumped even further. "I was here."

"How is that possible?" asked Sy.

"How was my performance?" Mac Q asked wryly.

"You were totally sick, like always," Ryder assured him.

A look of relief, and then of anger, crossed Mac Q's face. He pulled his hands up around his knees and starting rocking again. His eyes glazed over and lost their brief moment of clarity.

The boys looked at each other in horror, each with the same thought. What if the gargoyles had brought them here to clone them? And the Xanthia they'd seen . . . was it a clone waiting to replace her?

Ryder's eyes darted fearfully to Mac Q. "We've got to get out of here so we can warn the Council . . ." he whispered.

"How?" said Sy.

There was a clap of thunder, and Levi appeared, hovering in midair and looking cooler than ever. The Palooza Pixie's eyes were twinkling with excitement. "Hey, Ryder, how are you man? Hey . . . Sy, is it? Just wanted to run some catering ideas past you, Ryde; the party's coming up and I know how you looove your food . . ." He broke off midsentence, his face creasing in delight as he spotted Mac Q. "Congrats on your grammy!" he exclaimed. "Mac Q! Unbelievable! I didn't know you knew Mac Q," he accused Ryder, as if he should be personally advised of all of Ryder's acquaintances. "I dig you, man," he gushed. "Lower Realm music is where it's at! How about doing a live gig at my party . . .?"

"Levi!" shouted Ryder in desperation. "We need your help."

"That's Mac Q, man!" said Levi.

"Look, he can't see you, or hear you for that matter."

Levi looked offended. "You're not being helpful, Ryder. Anyway: gotta go—party business. Later . . ."

"*Wait*!" yelled Ryder and Sy.

Mac Q looked up at them, startled out of his rocking.

"Levi," said Ryder, exasperated. "Can you get us out of here? Dark elves and gargoyles dragged us here —" Speaking quickly, Ryder filled him in. "And not all of my powers are working," he said urgently.

"Well . . ." said Levi. "We can't have that. I mean, there's no way you're missing my party."

Ryder nodded to Mac Q. "What about him?"

"Leave him to me," said Levi calmly. "It will be an honor to help a legend like him. Where do you want to go?"

"Lower Realm. Manhattan, East Seventy-Ninth between Third and Lex," said Ryder.

Levi tapped them twice on the head and clicked his fingers. There was a loud *crack*. A second later they landed on the pavement at Seventy-Ninth Street, right outside Sy's townhouse. They looked at each other, smiling in relief, and sat on the steps to collect themselves before facing Sy's parents.

"Levi rocks!" said Sy.

"Yes, I'm finally glad he's been hassling me about his crazy party. I guess I'll have to go now—I owe him big time. He's awesome, Levi, but he's obsessed with celebrities." Ryder ran his hands through his hair. "I'm sure he's invited Dax and LB to his party—he won't be able to help himself, and I can't stand those guys."

Sy swallowed noisily. "I need to tell you something," he said.

"Shoot."

He told Ryder about Malibu. "I'm really sorry. I know how you and Xanthia feel about them. They used the information they got from me against our team. It's all my fault."

Ryder stood up. "I just lost my appetite," he said, his voice cold.

Sy's stomach was tight with disappointment. "Where are you going?"

Ryder hailed a cab. "See ya, Sy," he said, and took off.

12

The Dream Demons

Sy was even more disappointed when Ryder I.N.C.'d to tell him they'd canceled dinner. He'd told his grandfather about their terrifying encounter with the dark elves as soon as he got home. Samuel was understandably alarmed and insisted that Sy and Ryder meet with their Earth-tribe council representatives as soon as possible.

"Ryde —" Sy began.

"Gotta go," said Ryder and broke the connection.

Sy thought it would be almost impossible to sleep, but after the excitement of their adventure, he crashed.

* * *

He was glad he didn't have a chance to see anyone before he was told that his council leaders were expecting him, and Nudd led him to the initiation tent. Ryder was already there, polite but unfriendly, and they waited in an uncomfortable silence for Virgo, Taurus and Capricorn.

The boys stood respectfully when the council representatives entered. Sy had never seen them looking so serious and felt sure that Samuel had already worded them up. Virgo sat in a wide armchair facing the boys, Taurus and Capricorn soberly on either side of her.

"We understand that you have been through a very distressing experience," said Virgo gently. "Please share it with us to the best of your ability."

Sy cleared his throat nervously, but it was Ryder who took the lead. He launched into an account of their ordeal, starting with their ambush by the gargoyles and ending with how they'd been trapped in the laboratory and discovered Mac Q and the clones.

"Can you describe the liquid?" Capricorn asked.

"It was being pumped through tubes straight into the clones, even the infants," Ryder told him. "Black and thick . . . like tar."

"This is most concerning," said Capricorn.

After an hour of questions, they were allowed to go. Almost out of the tent, Ryder turned back. "I forgot my jacket," he said, and ran back. Sy followed, hoping for a chance to clear the air. At the door, they heard Taurus, Capricorn and Virgo speaking in hushed voices. Sy heard his name. He and Ryder strained forward to listen.

"Sy will need to know eventually," said Virgo. "It seems Incubus and the Darkforce have finally found a way to convert nightmares into substance. The liquid is accelerating the cloning process."

"Where do you think they are cultivating and storing it?" enquired Taurus.

"They may have amassed a large amount of the substance somewhere in the Lower Realm and camouflaged it in some way," said Capricorn. "With so much negativity around, it will be hard for us to pinpoint it. We'd surely sense it if it were in the Middle Realm."

"Taurus, they've tried to clone his team leader. They're getting desperate. You must watch Sy even more carefully," said Virgo.

"Who's there?" called Taurus sharply.

Ryder went in quickly and mumbled something about his jacket, scooped it up and left quickly, closing the door firmly behind him. He headed off to training without giving Sy a chance to talk to him.

Sy was filled with guilt and self-doubt. How could he have been so star struck that he let his own team down? As if major players like Dax and LB would be interested in him without an ulterior motive. He couldn't bring himself to go to training, and slouched off to his personal tent instead, avoiding everyone. He groaned—it was Levi's party tonight! Ryder would've told them what he'd done by now, and they wouldn't want him tagging along after that! Xanthia probably never wanted to speak to him again.

It was Raf who found him after training, wallowing in his own misery. "What's up?" he asked.

"I didn't mean for us to get disqualified."

Raf rolled his eyes. "Do you think you're the first person to be sucked in by the hype of celebrity? So you spent an amazing night, courtesy of two douches, and you said more than you should have. Xanthia understands—more than anyone, believe me. You need to get over it."

"But Ryder . . ."

"Ryder's had time to calm down. He knows you don't have the same history he has with those two."

"I can't face anyone."

"If you change your mind, we're in the Lounge," Raf said, and left him to it.

A bit later, Ryder turned up. He and Sy looked at each other and then away.

"I guess I over-reacted," Ryder admitted. "You couldn't have known what they're capable of."

"No, I messed up. I was star struck."

"You're too good for them," Ryder told him.

"I don't know about that," said Sy. "But their novelty has kinda worn off, if you know what I mean . . ."

Ryder smiled and held out his hand. Sy took it and they interlocked their thumbs in a warm handshake.

"Let's go," said Ryder. "I want to hear more about those French twins . . ."

* * *

Sy was greatly relieved that Ryder didn't hold a grudge—it seemed like their friendship was back on track. Now he only had Xanthia, Zak and Brady to face. They were waiting with Isobel for Levi to pick them up.

Xanthia looked amazing. She was wearing a white crocheted mini-dress with white frangipanis woven in her blonde hair. Her expression, however, belied her appearance. Raf seemed to be counseling her. "If it's too hard, then don't," he said gently.

"I promised Levi," she replied.

Ryder's expression hardened. Was she referring to him? What had he done wrong? How long would she keep giving him the cold shoulder?

Xanthia stayed close to Raf, not saying much. Sy thought he'd die of embarrassment. "Xanthia, I'm so sorry —"

She cut him off. "I hope it won't happen again."

He shook his head. "It won't."

"Taurus has told me that we'll have a chance to compete again next month, so let's just forget it and move on," she said.

The team surrounded him, and they each clapped him on the back and shoved him warmly; he was filled with immense relief.

Isobel gave him a quick hug. She, too, was looking very pretty and glamorous in tight black pants and a striped tank. She'd pinned her bangs back and her hazel eyes looked huge. It seemed to Sy that as soon as it had become clear that Ryder and Xanthia weren't a couple, Isobel had reverted back to her usual friendly self.

He wasn't sure if she was trying to make Ryder jealous or not, but she and Zak had really hit it off lately and seemed on the way to becoming a bit of an item.

"You look great," Ryder told her, meaning it.

"Thanks." Isobel beamed up at him.

"What's that?" said Sy, looking up.

A giant cube was moving quickly in the violet sky, heading to them. It landed, and dull thumping could be heard from within. The cube was massive, with pearly white walls, behind which they could see movement and flashes of color.

It opened into a grand formal entrance and the music belted out. The walls were transparent so those inside could see out, but Sy knew he hadn't been able to see in. Looking up, Sy could see at least five levels. Levi had really gone all out! A dancing crowd, largely pixies and other magical creatures, were jumping up and down in time to the beat. Sy counted at least three different DJs hovering above the crowd, taking it in turns to rev them up with the latest tracks. He smiled to himself when Mac Q's current hit blared.

Levi waved at them in delight. Wearing a new Prada pinstripe suit and a white beret, he pushed his way through a group of well-wishers, one arm slung around the real Mac Q, in the flesh! "Hey, all. You remember Mac Q. Are you ready to partee?"

Mac Q nodded at them from behind his dark shades.

"How can he see Levi and all this?" Sy asked Ryder, gesturing around him.

Ryder shrugged. "Levi's done some kind of magic, I guess."

"Happy birthday," said Sy, really wishing Levi all the best.

"Thanks, dude," said Levi. "You guys were the last pick-up. Where's Xanthia?"

"Over there," said Ryder.

Xanthia disappeared into the crowd with Levi, Mac Q and a large entourage following close behind. The rest of the team wandered around, soaking up the atmosphere, and wound up at a table overlooking the dance floor. Raf went to get them sodas. Outside became a blur, and moments later they were above the city of Manhattan at some kind of amusement park.

It looked as if Levi had hired out the entire park just for his party. Half the crowd streamed excitedly out of the cube, and Zak and Brady flowed out with them. There were rides across and through the tallest Manhattan buildings, and a massive rollercoaster wound its way through the skyscrapers at breakneck speed.

Sy wasn't the only one relieved to discover that Levi hadn't convinced Dax and LB to come to his party after all and, like Ryder, found his attention kept drifting back to Xanthia dancing with Mac Q on the dance floor. As she moved to the music, he was inching closer and closer to her.

Ryder stood up. "Let's dance," he said to Isobel. Eagerly, she put down her drink and took his hand.

"Here comes trouble," said Raf as Ryder led her away to dance.

Ryder positioned himself right near where Xanthia and Mac Q were dancing and pulled Isobel close. They danced for a few tracks before he led her to a shadowy corner and hooked up with her in front of everyone. Xanthia whispered something to Mac Q and they went outside to the amusement park.

The other boys rolled in. "That rollercoaster is brilliant!" Zak enthused. His face fell when he saw Isobel and Ryder kissing in the corner. "Bloody hell," he muttered.

The music stopped, and Levi announced to the delighted crowd that they would be attending the Teen Choice Awards after-party.

"I'm outta here," said Brady.

"It'll be fun!" encouraged Raf.

Brady shook his head. "I'll see you guys later."

The cube landed at the after-party, and those who were interested got out to mingle with their favorite celebs, knowing only active tribers or Triber-elite could see them.

"Hey, Sy!" Dax and LB waved him over. They were sitting at a booth near the dance floor, surrounded by a large entourage of admirers. And I used to want to be one of them, Sy thought wryly.

"Too bad about being disqualified," said Dax, his arm around a very pretty blonde girl. "But you can understand our position, right? You can't win by *cheating*."

LB grinned. "Sit down," he said.

"No thanks," said Sy. "I'm with my friends."

He walked away.

* * *

Sy was filling Raf and Zak in on his conversation with Dax and LB at the after-party buffet when Xanthia joined them. Isobel and Ryder had disappeared.

"Are you okay?" Raf asked.

She nodded, giving nothing away. Sy admired her poise.

Levi's party ended with a huge fireworks display and an enormous cake. By then, Sy had lost sight of the others. He thanked Levi for a great time and woke up in his bed shortly after.

It was almost a relief to go to school—like a vacation from the excitement of the Middle Realm. But one of his history classes involved writing up a family tree, and even though he couldn't show it, because no one would have understood what his problem was, it upset him. With everything that had been going on, he'd almost forgotten about Gabriel.

That night as he was getting ready for bed, he was filled with thoughts about his brother. He burned to know what was happening . . . and wished for the hundredth time that he could talk about the whole thing with his parents, but he'd be expelled from the tribe if he did and he just couldn't take that risk. As soon as he saw Ryder, he'd speak to him about starting up the hunt. He closed his eyes . . .

* * *

Gabriel was surfing. The waves were huge, crashing on the sandbank. Sy couldn't see his face, but he knew it was him. His brother was caught in the middle of the impact zone, about to get smashed by the next set of waves. Sy held his breath, but Gabriel just made it over the top of a huge peak and Sy watched with pride as he rode wave after perfect wave. He was having so much fun, and Sy's heart swelled at the sight of him . . . until the sparkling turquoise water turned black and thick and Sy's heart beat faster. Gabriel was standing alone on the familiar island of land, frantically trying to save himself from being drowned in the tar-like substance as it gushed thickly toward him.

The shrieks of terror were loud and piercing, and Sy was afraid. He wanted to help! Despite his terror, Gabriel seemed desperate to pass on a message; he was holding something in his hand. Sy knew it was significant. He strained to see, but again all he could make out was some type of golden device.

An alarm sounded. Sy woke up, his heart thumping. A siren was blaring outside his window. He sat up, turned on his light, and thought he caught the hint of a black shadow glide out his window. He got up to look, but there was nothing there.

He'd been dreaming about Gabriel; he could feel it, but the details were sketchy. He pulled open his bed-side drawer and found a notepad and pen, spending some time trying to remember, but could only manage to jot down a few details. Frustrated, he gave up, turned over and fell into a restless sleep.

* * *

Sy met Ryder in the Lounge, feeling a vague sense of loss and anguish. "How's it going?" he asked, aware that Ryder was having his own issues.

"I'm in a messy situation," Ryder admitted. "I could do with the distraction, so shoot."

Ryder listened, his face creasing in a frown as Sy tried but failed to remember anything about the dream beyond what he'd written down. "All I know is that he's trying to show me something, but I don't know what," Sy said, desperate.

"Sy, I think your dream was stolen."

"You mean one of Incubus's dream demons?" asked Sy, feeling alarmed at the memory of the black shadow near his window. "How do they do it?"

Ryder didn't know. "You know when you wake

up suddenly and then roll over and go into a different dream?" he asked. "That's because your dream was stolen."

"But I've remembered heaps of my dreams," said Sy.

"The ones you remember haven't been stolen."

A plan began to form in Sy's mind.

"The demon is long gone," said Ryder, reading Sy's thoughts and wanting to set him straight. "Incubus is dangerous."

"I've just got this crazy strong feeling that the dream that's been stolen is the best chance I've got to find my brother . . . I need to get that dream. That vision I had was real, and I've *got* to work out what Gabriel was trying to tell me. I have to save him."

"Sy, you know I'm up for just about anything, but retrieving a dream has never been done before. Samuel couldn't even keep up with a demon."

"I have to try," said Sy. His voice rose as his frustration bubbled to the surface. "I can't keep pretending I don't have a brother, and no one will tell me *anything*!" He put his head in his hands.

Ryder sat there thinking for a while, and Sy thought he'd burst with the tension.

"It's not going to be easy," Ryder sighed. "But I'll help you."

13

The Sleep Custodians

Sy and Ryder met in Ryder's tent after training. "I found out from my Grandpa that Incubus has hidden the *Book of Dreams* somewhere in the Lower Realm. Even if by some miracle we find it, it'll be guarded with tighter security than the White House," said Ryder. "Grandpa reckons the book will have trillions of dreams in it. It'll be virtually impossible to find yours, *and* we risk getting trapped inside . . ." Ryder paused, giving Sy time to digest what he was saying. "Maybe we should think about other ways to find your brother," he suggested gently.

"*No*! This is the best chance I have of finding him. I'm going to get back my dream with or without your help," said Sy stubbornly.

"Okay, okay," said Ryder. "Just don't say I didn't warn you. We need to meet with Asta from the Sleep Custodians. They invented the *Book of Dreams* and have been trying to recover it for the last thousand years. Asta and her family are direct descendants of the original architects of the book. I can't ask Grandpa any more questions. If he knew what we were up to, he'd freak! If we mention him, though, I think she'll see us. They were good friends; there's a photo of the two of them at our place."

Sy remembered her—the warrior-like woman who had caught his attention.

Ryder I.N.C.'d the Sleep Custodians. As soon as he mentioned he was Samuel's grandson, they were granted an appointment with Asta.

"Let's go," said Sy excitedly, feeling charged. He was finally on the way to finding his brother!

* * *

The Custodian Kingdom was located in the Middle Realm, above the rainforest of the Amazon jungle in Brazil. They couldn't find any information on the I.N.C., but they managed to find a picture of it in the Knowledge tent and jumped straight in, landing at the edge of the jungle. They had read that magical protection around the Kingdom would prevent them from teleporting any closer.

It was humid. The jungle was humming with the sounds of nocturnal animals. As they flew up the Amazon River, Sy shivered at the thought of the piranhas that he knew were lurking beneath its surface . . .

A group of warriors loomed out of the darkness.

They were brown-skinned women with caramel-colored eyes that slanted upward, accentuating their high cheekbones and pointy chins; and they had long hair that reached their navels. They weren't tall, but with their lean, athletic frames sparsely dressed for the heat, their self-assured presence was intimidating. Sy and Ryder shared a glance: these must be the Custodians.

One stepped forward. "We will escort you the rest of the way," she said.

They traveled up the river, increasing their altitude until the darkness melted away, revealing a well-guarded fortress city that seemed to be made entirely of gold and crystal. Buildings of various sizes shimmered in the violet sky, all facing a larger structure that towered over the others; circular in shape, its domed roof was made of giant crystals interconnected with gold. Groups of Custodian warriors stood under the arches that formed the perimeter of the city.

"That must be the palace," whispered Ryder.

The city stretched for miles. They flew over a group of younger-looking warriors practicing martial arts techniques. Eventually, their party descended, heading to the palace's main entrance. They passed through a magnificent doorway in the crystal dome, and landed.

Inside, narrow steps led down several flights to a short corridor. The floor was encrusted with turquoise stones, threaded with black. It was impressive. They stopped at a heavy wooden door, with warrior guards on either side. The Custodians who had accompanied them departed silently, and the guards unlocked the grand double doors.

Asta was waiting for them. Her brown skin was glowing and she wore an elaborate gold silk gown, her honey-blonde hair braided and coiled elegantly around her head. Sy thought she was breathtaking.

"Welcome, Joshua and Sy. Would you join me for some tea?" Her voice was soft and sounded like music.

Ryder and Sy nodded nervously and sat at the table where preparations for an elaborate tea ceremony had already commenced. Various herbs, spices, flowers and elixirs were mixed, ground and cooked. Even the water was run through an elaborate filtration process.

Ryder cleared his throat. "Thank you for seeing us," he said politely. "We were hoping you could talk to us about the *Book of Dreams*."

"You are Samuel Ryderson's grandson, isn't that right?" Asta asked him.

Ryder nodded.

"You have your grandfather's eyes, and also his ability to get straight to the point," she said, smiling fondly. "I don't mind admitting that many of my fellow Custodians were quite taken with him in the old days—before he married your grandmother, of course," she confided. "Does he know that you are here?"

"Not exactly," said Ryder, shifting uncomfortably.

"My dream was stolen by a dream demon and I need to get it back," Sy interjected, sensing Ryder's hesitation. This was his time to assert himself. "It was about my brother, Gabriel. Who I've never met . . . The dream is my only clue," he explained. His heart sank—it even sounded to himself like he was babbling.

"Have some tea," Asta offered, pouring the steaming liquid into their cups. Sy took a cautious sip. It tasted like cinnamon and flowers. "It's made with over one hundred ingredients, all natural leaves and herbs found in the Amazon," said Asta.

"It's very good," said Ryder.

"But you haven't come for our excellent tea." Asta's expression grew suddenly serious. "You know the dangers associated with retrieving a stolen dream from the book. Our palace is filled with portraits of Custodian warriors who have attempted to recover the Book, and never returned."

"This is something I have to do," said Sy earnestly.

Asta poured herself more tea. After a pause, she said, "I see that you are very determined." She smiled at Ryder. "And I would like to help Samuel's grandson."

She settled herself. "Let me start from the beginning . . .

"The *Book of Dreams* was invented by my people five thousand years ago to record a copy of every dream. Dreams can help you to discover more about yourself and your purpose. They can assist you to overcome the personal challenges you will face throughout your life," she said.

"For five thousand years those in the Lower and Middle Realms enjoyed the benefits of being able to recall their dreams. You simply had to wish for the dream and it would be placed in your memory. Each individual's ability to recall a dream varies; the desire and intention must be pure for the dream to be provided back to the dreamer."

She paused and sipped her tea. "Our community became known as the Custodians because we nurtured the Book and continued to explore new ways to help people connect with their dreams." Her face darkened. "A thousand years ago an evil sorcerer, Incubus, stole the Book and used dark magic to corrupt it. The Book still records a copy of every dream, but Incubus prevented people from remembering the truth about their dreams, filling them with despair and negativity instead." She leaned forward. "More and more people began to have nightmares."

"Could someone access their dream if they were inside the Book?" asked Sy.

"A connection always remains between a dream and its dreamer. If you were able to get inside the Book and knew the date and time of your dream, then yes," replied Asta. "The rightful owner has the ability to decode their dream. Once it is decoded, it is automatically placed in your memory. But Incubus patrols the Book. If you encounter him, he can trap you inside your own mind—placing you in a permanent dream-state. He can tamper with your sense of reality and confuse you with the dream you most wish to see. People get so excited that their fantasy has finally come true, they subconsciously resist waking up.

"After a while your dream-state becomes your new reality and you are a prisoner inside your own dream, unable to return to the Lower Realm. Incubus feeds off people's fears and phobias. He can also trap you in your all-time worst nightmare—and he will, because Incubus draws power from every dream he controls."

Sy hated to admit it, even to himself, but their mission seemed suicidal. They had no idea how they would get into the Book, let alone get out of it when so many before them had failed.

Asta swirled her lukewarm tea and studied their earnest faces thoughtfully. "Custodians seem to be more susceptible to Incubus, perhaps because we are so closely connected to the Book." She continued to study them silently for a few moments, as if she were contemplating an important decision. Finally she exhaled and narrowed her caramel-colored eyes. "Perhaps you can do what we have long failed to achieve."

She put down her cup and held them with her eyes. "But I must warn you, the Book is aligned with the divine wisdom of the cosmos. There are only certain times in the course of the stars that the Golden Seal in the Heart of the Book can be accessed, even by the greatest of Custodians. This time is now, which also encourages me that there is some higher destiny in your coming to me with this quest. But beware: the window is small and will not come again for another forty years. You must achieve your quest before the Pisces full moon."

She sat back and appraised them. "Are you prepared to take the risk?"

"I am," said Sy. He swallowed, his heart pounding, almost afraid to look at Ryder. He sagged with relief when he heard Ryder clear his throat and say, "Yeah, me too, I guess."

Asta handed Ryder a flat turquoise disk, no bigger than a quarter. "This is an original prototype of the Book. It will help you to find your way around and translate ancient Custodian inscriptions."

She gave Sy a transparent bag made of the finest gold silk, with a plaited gold-and-turquoise drawstring. "This is sacred magic dust taken from the Heart of the Book. It will help you open doors that are locked, and may help you get out of dangerous situations. You must be in the Heart of the Book to defeat Incubus. We believe he has been unable to influence the Heart and that it still remains protected by our enchantments. You will be safer there."

"How will we know where the Heart of the Book is?" asked Sy.

"Open the golden door. Take exactly eighteen steps and you will be inside the Heart." Asta taught them the ancient Custodian command to open the door. "Not all your tribal powers will work inside the Book, but you will be able to fly. You must retrieve your dream before you are due to return to the Lower Realm or you will remain trapped inside forever," she warned. A clock chimed in the distance.

Asta rose to her feet. Their meeting was over. She smiled, rather sadly. "I wish you the best of luck!"

They were able to teleport straight back to base-camp where things were hotting up for the upcoming lunar festival. "If I'm going to die in the *Book of Dreams*," said Ryder, "I sure hope I get to lead my team to victory first! You really need to win this one, Sy. Our tribe's reputation is at stake!"

Sy's stomach tightened. He exhaled nervously.

"No pressure or anything," Ryder said quickly. Freaking Sy out would not help. "You just won't be able to do anything about the Book until after the festival."

"Yeah, I hear you," said Sy. "I really do want to win this one. And Ryder—you are not going to die!"

As they headed off to training, Sy prayed that he was right.

14

Perception Prism

The approaching lunar festival was Virgo: Earth-tribe's month.

"Okay team, we're competing again," Xanthia told them during an intense training session. "After considering the protest from Fire-tribe, the Council decided that the same four teams will compete again." She looked at them one by one. "That means we're up against Dax and LB."

"Bloody hell!" said Zak.

"Exactly." Xanthia smiled. "This is our chance to prove we can win with excellent preparation and superior skill. I'm going to push us all extra hard. Take things to the next level. Everyone okay with that?"

They nodded their agreement.

She developed a rigorous schedule for them. Over the next few training sessions, Sy watched her push herself both physically and mentally. Following her lead, he exerted himself beyond what he would have thought he was capable of. Sy had something to prove to himself and his team. It was his fault they had lost the last challenge, and he wanted to make it up to them. He was grateful for Raf, whose humor was a kind of balance and kept the sessions fun—most of the time . . .

They focused on practicing standard Earth-tribe powers; concentrating on Earth Blend, Tree Teleporting and Shadow Concealment. They also worked on perfecting their martial arts and forcefields. All of these would be useful, both as a way to beat their opponents and as a defense. Xanthia also stressed the importance of mental stamina: remaining calm and level-headed if the unexpected happened. The likelihood of being ambushed was high, and no one wanted a repeat performance of what Dax and LB had done to the Water-tribe in the last challenge.

Raf volunteered his free time to help Sy work on his powers. He still couldn't fully master his Shadow Concealment power. Nothing Raf said seemed to help the mental block he had . . . he couldn't stand the thought of being trapped in a small place.

* * *

The day of the festival had arrived. Earth-tribe gathered by their mighty symbol, waiting to be teleported. Ryder pushed his way through the crowd to wish Sy's team luck. He shook hands with Brady and Zak, and clapped Raf and Sy on the back. "Good luck, Xanthe," he said formally, touching her gently on her shoulder.

"Thank you," she replied.

When they locked eyes, Sy could feel the electricity between them. When Xanthia took a step toward Ryder, Sy was pretty sure he wasn't the only one in the team holding his breath.

Taurus approached and the moment was lost. Raf rolled his eyes.

"Ready?" Taurus asked her kindly.

Xanthia nodded and waited to be teleported with her team.

As soon as everyone was in the stadium, the Ringmaster appeared. "Welcome to the Council . . ." He bowed to the Zodiac Council, and then encompassed the crowd. "And welcome to all! We celebrate the month of Virgo." The Earth-tribe section cheered loudly. "You are about to witness a special festival," he continued, raising his powerful arms. "The task will be particularly challenging as it is a rematch. Good luck to the participating teams: you know who you are . . . and now, please make yourself comfortable and enjoy the entertainment . . ."

When the entertainment was over, a hush fell over the stadium. The Ringmaster raised his platinum staff. "*Select*!" he commanded.

Sy thought he was prepared this time, but it was still a shock when the green light hit him in the chest.

He was teleported to the center platform with the other teams.

There was a lot of tension during the lap around the stadium. This was the first time Sy had seen Dax and LB since the after-party. They ignored him, focusing their attention on Xanthia. They tried to physically intimidate her and undermine her composure, blocking her path, towering over her and staring her down.

"Leave her alone," Dana from Air-tribe called out to them as the Earth team stood around Xanthia protectively. Sy's eyes narrowed suspiciously. Was Dax hiding something? There was a blur of movement. Was it his imagination, or had Sy just seen a small dart fly from Dax's palm?

Xanthia grabbed at her throat and choked back a little scream of alarm. "Ow," she said. "What was that?"

"I think you might've been hit with a dart," said Sy. "I saw Dax —"

Xanthia pulled herself together and showed them her throat. "Do you see anything?"

They looked, but there was no wound. If it *had* been a dart, it seemed to have disappeared.

"Are you sure?" Raf asked Sy.

Sy shook his head. "It happened so quick, but I'm pretty sure . . ."

"Should we pull out?" asked Brady.

Xanthia was adamant. "*No!*" She showed them her neck again. "Look, it's fine; there's nothing there."

The Ringmaster addressed the audience. "This month's challenge is the Perception Prism. It's a dangerous challenge. The last time the Council gave us permission to use the prism was over fifty years ago." The Earth and Fire sections of the stadium cheered loudly. "And we shall monitor the action very closely this time."

The Fire-tribers roared and stamped their feet, but the rest of the stadium was quiet.

"Bloody brilliant," said Zak sarcastically, under his breath.

Xanthia's face reddened and Sy felt his stomach lurch sickeningly. Brady shared a queasy smile that was more of a grimace.

"Don't worry about it," said Raf, winking at them. "No one will care about all that when we win."

The Ringmaster waved his hands, and four spinning crystal prisms appeared midair, each one coming to a stop in front of its respective tribe. As they spun, the edges reflected the shining Northern Star, sending multi-colored rays of light flashing around the stadium.

"Inside the prism, each tribe will be faced with a challenge from an opposing element," the Ringmaster explained. "Earth with Air, Water with Fire. Each team will need to work together and overcome obstacles that the elements will throw at you, while searching for the opposing element's tribal symbol.

You will compete —" he paused for dramatic effect, "without your five senses."

The stadium erupted with nervous and excited chatter. The Ringmaster silenced them with a commanding gesture. "Team members will lose each sense at different times throughout the challenge. When one sense is taken away, another will be returned. You must work together to be successful." He raised his hands dramatically. "Let the challenge begin!"

Sy and the rest of Earth-tribe team were teleported into the prism. Within an instant, the prism walls disappeared and all they could see was endless violet sky, with dark storm clouds approaching. A second later everything plunged into darkness.

"Hey," Sy said, panicking. "I can't see."

"You've lost your sight," said Raf. "It'll come back soon. Grab hold of each other so we stick together."

"I think I've just lost my hearing," called Zak, loudly.

Sy was relieved when his sight returned, but had to admit he didn't like what he saw: Xanthia's eyes lacked their usual clarity; she seemed distracted.

"Okay," she said. "I've just lost my sight. Brady, you lead us away from the clouds."

Maybe she was just nervous, Sy thought. Everyone was apprehensive, on edge as they tried to prepare for the hurdles that would be placed before them.

The menacing clouds moved quickly, blocking out

the shining light, and they were caught in a real storm. Huge raindrops pelted down. Their protective gear shielded them from the wet but couldn't control the wind. It was so turbulent that they had trouble flying in a straight line. Lightning sizzled nearby.

Raf pointed to his ears. He must've lost his hearing. He gestured madly at two giant black clouds headed straight for them. Inside the clouds, visibility was poor. They clung to each other desperately as they tried to fly through them.

Zak, caught in an air pocket, lost his grip and dropped down out of sight. The others watched helplessly as his screams were drowned by the roar of the wind.

Earth team panicked. Brady clearly couldn't hear a thing and Raf was almost crushing Sy, holding on without a proper sense of touch. Sy looked to Xanthia. "What should we do?"

Her sight had returned, but she just stared at him blankly. She looked dazed.

Brady chimed in: "Xanthia?"

She kept touching her neck and didn't respond to any of their requests for instructions. Sy felt like he was falling and clutched at Brady. He'd obviously just lost his sense of touch.

The Earth-tribe team was in trouble . . .

* * *

Ryder watched on, feeling apprehensive. Xanthia did not seem like her usual competent self. Next to him, Isobel was pale and was muttering to herself in French. This was the most dangerous challenge they had ever witnessed. And it wasn't just Earth-tribe . . .

The Water-tribe was stuck in a giant volcano, which was spitting molten lava. One member of their team was desperately gripping the edge of a rock, inches away from falling into a river of crimson flames.

The Fire-tribe looked like they were about to drown in a major tidal wave. Despite his anxiety, Ryder experienced a brief moment of satisfaction as he watched Dax and LB out of their depth for once.

The entire stadium was deathly quiet, the spectators on the edge of their seats . . .

* * *

For Sy, losing his sight was the most debilitating. Flying without vision was difficult, and he had to rely totally on his sonar ability. But the most disturbing thing was that Xanthia was letting them down. She'd stopped midair and wouldn't move, oblivious to the pulling and encouragement of the others. No matter how hard they tried, she wouldn't budge.

Raf stepped up to the role of substitute team leader, exhibiting patience and good lateral thinking. "I think I spotted the Air-tribe symbol in the eye of the storm," he shouted. "Be prepared for anything from Air-tribe."

With Brady's help, Raf created an earth tunnel that led them into the eye of the storm which raged all around them, but without Xanthia's strength, it was weak and sections crumbled under their feet. They linked arms, dragging Xanthia with them. The sky just kept getting darker.

"Look out!" shouted Brady.

Out of a dark cloud, a squadron formation of Air-tribers attacked. The Earth-triber's tunnel smashed after being hit by a series of powerful air-ball blasts. Air team divided and, using their bodies, created swirling twisters to block the path to the Air symbol.

The Earth team tried valiantly to create a force-field to limit the impact of the twisters, but without Zak and Xanthia's fields, it collapsed. Xanthia was hit by a powerful bolt of lightning and disappeared. The remaining three scattered in the intense wind as they spun out of control.

* * *

Ryder's heart sank as he watched Air team claim the Earth-tribe symbol without Xanthia's team even offering them a challenge. Earth-tribe had been on the back foot from the beginning, and now they'd been soundly crushed.

He was deafened by cheers from the Fire- and Water-tribe sections. Their teams were neck and neck, and it was anyone's game. Water-tribe had found the Fire symbol and were scaling the inside walls of a volcano, avoiding the occasional explosions which prevented them from flying. They were about to emerge from the top.

Ryder might hate Dax and LB, but he had to admit that Fire-tribe were showing amazing teamwork and resilience. They'd created a giant fire sphere that fully encased the team. This allowed them to safely pass through a tidal wave to retrieve the Water symbol. They all used the same wave to surf back on surfboards made of fire. They reached the shore and looked up expectantly.

Fire-tribe had won.

The prisms disappeared and teams were transported back to the stadium, Earth-tribe landing in an exhausted, tangled heap. All the other competitors were returned to the stadium, looking worse for wear, but safe.

The Ringmaster made a short speech and presented a medallion to Air-tribe and a golden moon to the Fire-tribe team. The Fire-tribers roared their appreciation. Dax and LB were jubilant. They locked eyes with Xanthia and raised their trophies to her spitefully.

She looked shattered.

Back at basecamp, Sy sat with his team, feeling their misery and confusion. They were all embarrassed by their performance, but Xanthia was mortified. Sy guessed she wasn't used to under-achieving.

"I'm so sorry, Zak—that must have been awful for you. And thanks, Raf, for everything. I take full responsibility for our loss," she said. "I let you all down. Some team leader I am . . ." She choked up and couldn't finish.

"I think Dax did throw a dart at you," said Raf. "You were drugged, or something, so stop being so hard on yourself."

"I never got back the senses that I lost," she admitted. "And my head felt like it had been poleaxed!"

"I knew we should have pulled out," said Brady.

"You're right," Xanthia said. "I'm sorry."

"There wasn't any mark or anything," said Zak. "It would have been pretty weird to pull out without any real reason."

"It was my fault," said Xanthia. "I knew something was wrong—I just really wanted to compete. I was stubborn and it put you all in danger."

* * *

Ryder wasn't surprised to find them all huddling in Xanthia's tent. "Mind if I join you?" he asked uncertainly. His heart jumped. As soon as she saw him, Xanthia got up and hugged him. Then she burst into tears. He held her tightly. "What happened to you?"

Sy told him about the dart, and a hot rush of anger washed over him.

"I've heard Dax and LB are in serious trouble,

and this might explain it," he said. "They deserve to be banished from the tribe." Ryder touched Xanthia's throat gently, and then cursed under his breath. "They're going to pay for that," he vowed.

From the corner of his eye, Ryder saw Raf and Zak smirking at each other.

"Do you want to come to my tent for a while?" Ryder asked Xanthia.

She nodded, wiping her eyes. "Is that all right with you guys?"

Raf rolled his eyes dramatically. "Sure," he said.

Ryder put his arm around her, and they walked quietly back to his tent. She told him about her experience in the challenge, and he inspected her throat again. "That sounds horrible, but it looks okay now," he said.

"I'm sorry about the silent treatment," Xanthia said. "After Dax . . . I'm just not up for another player." She looked at him, her blue eyes darkening like they always did when she was really serious.

Ryder wanted to protest that he was nothing like Dax, but after what he'd done, he couldn't. "There's nothing between me and Isobel," he said. "We're just friends."

"Does she know that?"

The silence stretched between them.

"Make it right, and then we'll talk," Xanthia told him. She smiled, leaned over to kiss him on the cheek, and left.

161

15

Stealing Dreams

It was mid-fall and Halloween was round the corner. Rebecca was frantically planning her menu and guest list for Thanksgiving. This year she had invited Samuel and Ryder to join them. "I'll do the candy shopping for Halloween," Sy offered. "And help Dad get the house ready for the trick-or-treaters." He figured it wouldn't kill him to make an effort at home, considering the massive secret he was keeping from his parents.

There was much to feel optimistic about. His Level-1 training was progressing well, and his martial arts skills were getting better each week. Learning how to use the sonar abilities was really difficult. They practiced blindfolded and had to judge distance and make it through challenging obstacle courses. He'd almost mastered the Shadow Concealment power, thanks to the extra time Raf had spent with him, and was looking forward to receiving his first light-spectrum color in the next lunar month.

Sy's confidence was improving, and people were noticing. Some of the coolest kids at school had started inviting him to hang out with them. In the Middle Realm he was surprised and pleased when he was included in a conversation between Ryder and Raf in the Lounge, where Ryder opened up for the first time about his relationship dramas.

"I've apologized to Isobel," Ryder told them, after ordering shrimp dumplings.

"Good," said Raf, continuing the Chinese theme and ordering a beef and noodle stir fry. "It wasn't fair to treat her like that. You knew she was into you after the last time you hooked up with her."

"Only once before, and it was New Year's," said Ryder, a little defensive. "It was no big deal."

"Not to you," Raf said, pulling his wooden chopsticks apart.

"Aren't you going to eat anything?" Ryder asked Sy with his mouth full.

Sy shook his head. "I'm not hungry. So what did Isobel say?"

"She's upset. Cursed at me in French. But I think she'll come around," said Ryder. "Can I please get some spring rolls?"

"She's spending a lot of time with Zak," Sy told them. "I think he likes her."

"Bloody Zak," said Ryder fondly, dipping his spring rolls in chili salsa. "I hope they get together so she can get off my case."

163

Raf helped himself to a spring roll. "Has anyone heard anything more about Dax and LB?"

"No," said Ryder. "I wanted to go to Taurus, but we have no proof."

"I think we need to take matters into our own hands," said Raf.

Their palms began the sixty-second countdown, and they agreed to reconvene to work out a plan.

* * *

A few days later, after a particularly good training session, Ryder met up with Sy in the Entertainment tent. After an hour of blowing up vicious zombies, Ryder stretched and grinned. "It's time to take on some dream demons for real, Sy," he said.

Sy was thrilled; he'd been quietly stressing about running out of time to access the Golden Seal in the Heart of the Book. He felt pretty sure that finding a demon would be easy now that they'd made the decision to start . . .

But he was wrong! They spent two weeks circling the streets of Manhattan and the surrounding boroughs with no luck.

After another missed training session and failed search, the boys slid into a booth at a triber-friendly café in West Broadway. "I don't know about you, but I'm beginning to think the dream demons are invisible," said Ryder. He ordered them chocolate shakes. "Maybe you didn't even see one at your place."

"I did see one," Sy insisted, although secretly he wondered whether Ryder was right.

Their waitress placed two frosted glasses and extra-thick shakes on the table. "Anything else I can get you?" she asked.

Sy was about to say no, but Ryder said, "I'm starving," and ordered pastrami on rye with a side order of fries and coleslaw. Sy watched him eat, wondering if he'd ever find Gabriel.

Why could he remember some dreams and not others? He sat up in his chair. "I've just worked out how to find a dream demon! We've been looking in all the wrong places," he said impatiently, nudging Ryder to get his attention. "We need to go where a dream demon is guaranteed to visit . . ."

"Like where?" asked Ryder, tuning in.

"Like my friend, Oliver's. He told me that he has never ever remembered a dream," said Sy. "I bet they're all getting stolen!"

"I hope your hunch is right, Sy. It's crazy wasting time just flying around."

The next night they skipped training and flew to Oliver's place in New Jersey. It was a two-story weatherboard house, painted white with blue shutters. They saw lights on at two open windows; hip hop drifted out of one, and they heard girls singing loudly.

"His sisters," whispered Sy. "Let's check out the other window."

Oliver was sitting at his desk, diligently bent over his laptop. "I don't know how he concentrates with all that noise," said Ryder. He pointed to a large oak outside Oliver's bedroom window. "Let's wait over there."

They got comfortable on a solid branch midway up the tree. After a couple of hours, a goblin appeared out of the shadows, startling Sy. He had a baseball cap on backward, and the name "MIKE" glowed on his red tank in silver letters. Surprisingly muscular for such a small fellow, he was perched on what looked to Sy like a cross between a snowboard and a skateboard with a trailer attached. "Goblins Express—Fresh Pizzas Delivered Fast" was emblazoned on the side of the trailer in red and silver letters.

"Right on time," said Ryder. "Impressive."

"Two large pizzas with the lot—extra pepperoni," said the goblin in a businesslike manner, reaching into the trailer and pulling out two boxes. "Name and tribe?" he asked.

"Josh Ryderson, Earth."

"Have a pleasant evening." The goblin revved his hover board noisily and sped off into the night.

"Cool, I'm starving," said Sy, helping himself to a slice of steaming pizza and taking a bite. "It's so good."

"That's just how I roll," said Ryder, looking pleased.

"How do you pay?" said Sy with his mouth full.

"You don't. Earth-tribe picks up the tab. One of the perks of being a triber," said Ryder.

"Awesome," said Sy, and bit into his slice.

They ate in silence, enjoying the pizza and keeping a close eye on Oliver's room.

It was heading toward midnight and Sy was feeling cramped. The music had stopped, and Oliver finally turned off his bedroom light. All was silent except for some neighborhood cats out on the prowl.

Ryder sat upright. He pointed excitedly. "Look!"

A black mist appeared from the shadows and glided into Oliver's room. If they weren't looking out for it, they would have missed it. Slowly, carefully, they flew to the window and peered in. The black mist had transformed itself into a dark, emaciated creature that was opaquely transparent. It moved toward where Oliver was sleeping peacefully and raised its bony index finger to Oliver's face. A long, needle-like device extended from its nail . . .

They watched transfixed as the demon lifted Oliver's eyelid, plunged the needle into his pupil and held it there for a few seconds. Sy winced. The needle-thing was long enough to go directly into Oliver's brain; but throughout it all, Oliver remained motionless, in a deep sleep, only twitching slightly when the needle entered his eye.

Apparently successful, the demon withdrew the probe, left the bed and turned into a black mist again, heading to the window where Ryder and Sy were spying. "Quick, the tree," whispered Ryder urgently.

They Blended with a nearby oak and vanished from view. The demon floated to the next house. Ryder had to wait a few anxious minutes for Sy to recover from the Blend before they could follow.

The dream demon was flying purposefully around the neighborhood, but Sy and Ryder couldn't detect any kind of pattern to the choices it made. It flew into two houses in a row, but then skipped right by the next five houses, went into one and skipped two. Sy wondered why poor Oliver was hit so regularly. He grimaced. "That giant needle would have gone in my eye the night I dreamed about my brother," he said.

"I know," said Ryder. "I was just wondering how many times I've been hit."

The demon moved like a panther, a professional nocturnal predator. Finally, it seemed to have achieved its quota for the evening and flew toward the black clouds. Sy and Ryder were on its tail, but having trouble keeping up with its incredible speed. Sy started to feel a little dizzy and disorientated. He'd never gone this fast before. "Hold onto my feet," Ryder yelled. "He's getting away!"

Sy gratefully grabbed Ryder's ankles and shut his eyes tight as they climbed to an even higher altitude and flew even faster. There weren't many tribers who could beat Ryder on speed . . .

The demon passed through a shimmering wall in the sky, and Ryder and Sy followed, desperate not to lose him. It felt like they'd been drenched in icy water. "What was that?" Sy asked nervously. He looked down but his clothes were dry.

"Dunno," said Ryder, looking around. "I think we passed through some kind of portal." He sped on.

The demon finally slowed its pace and descended quickly. As they got closer, they saw palm trees clustered along a winding river. Several crocodiles lay lazily, their tails swishing in the mud.

The demon veered west toward a vast space where triangular structures jutted from the landscape. They were flying over a desert; the buildings were pyramids. They were in Egypt! They entered a deserted valley. After many turns and twists, they spotted a lone, slightly lopsided pyramid set apart from the others. Next to it, an ancient temple was almost buried in the sand. The demon disappeared inside the pyramid.

"What should we do now?" Sy asked.

"Wait," said Ryder, his senses on high alert.

What looked like giant black rain clouds swept into view and they shrank back. With horror they saw it was not clouds but hundreds of demons gliding in sync to the pyramid, where they promptly disappeared.

When they'd gathered their courage, Sy and Ryder flew cautiously toward the great structure.

"Should we go in?" Sy asked, half hoping Ryder would say no.

Ryder was quiet, thinking. "For a few seconds, just to check it out," he said. "But stay close."

They squeezed themselves into a small slit near the top. It smelled damp and musty. Slivers of light from the moon filtered through the many cracks. There were hundreds of demons inside—and yet, no sound! The demons did not speak nor acknowledge each another. They moved in a trance, as if they too were dreaming. The silence was threatening.

When each demon came to a stop, it transformed from mist into the opaque creature they had seen at Oliver's. It was creepy to see so many of them in the one place, their ghostlike forms shimmering in the semi-darkness. They watched with fascinated interest: the minute a demon transformed itself, a large square panel on the pyramid's dusty stone floor turned transparent, and it glided straight through.

"Where are they all going?"

Sy had forgotten to whisper, and Ryder elbowed him furiously as several demons paused, looking around blindly. After a few tense seconds, they continued their vanishing under the pyramid floor. Sy and Ryder exhaled in relief.

"Let's take a closer look," whispered Ryder.

Their backs firmly pressed against the cool limestone wall, they descended slowly. The elaborate inscriptions on the walls made Sy wonder if an ancient pharaoh was buried inside.

"They're depositing the dreams," whispered Ryder, watching the floor closely when it turned transparent. "That's it! The *Book of Dreams* is buried under the pyramid!"

Something flew past Ryder's face. He put his hand up instinctively and felt whatever it was brush past his fingers. Trying not to panic, Ryder nudged Sy and silently indicated that they should move away. They ascended slowly and squeezed into an indentation in the stone. Ryder frowned, and squinted to see whether he could catch a glimpse of what had brushed past him.

He almost gagged with revulsion; the floor of the pyramid was infested with oversized silver scorpions with gigantic razor-sharp pincers, their long tails raised, half-coiled assertively. They flew around boldly, hundreds of them glowing in the darkened chamber.

Sy's whole body stiffened. He and Ryder shrank against the wall in terror. Barely breathing, and too scared to move, they watched as the demons went about their business, unaffected by the scorpions, which buzzed around them aggressively, some going right through their misty bodies as they attempted to strike. The lack of a viable target wound them up to a mad frenzy.

"Let's get out of here," whispered Ryder.

Sy nodded, and inch-by-inch they made their way to the top of the pyramid, exhaling in relief as they breathed the cool night air. They could not even imagine entering the pyramid again and facing those scorpions. Sy began to seriously doubt that he would ever be able to get his dream back.

"Maybe we should speak to Xanthia and the others?" suggested Ryder. "Get everyone's heads together."

"But I've never told them about Gabriel," Sy said, not wanting to admit that he didn't really want to.

"I don't think we have a choice," said Ryder. "It's too dangerous for us to keep it to ourselves."

* * *

The next lunar festival came and went. Much to the great disappointment of the others, there was no chance to confront Dax and LB, as they did not attend.

Air-tribe won the challenge, thanks to their superior flying skills. Sy and Zak decided they much preferred watching the challenges to participating in them.

After the challenge, Sy and Zak headed to the Lounge. Xanthia and Isobel were sitting together near the entrance, engrossed in an intense conversation. A few moments later they stood up and hugged.

"Good," said Zak, sounding pleased.

"What's that about?" asked Sy as they sat at a different table, and he ordered a soda.

"Xanthia wanted to clear the air with Isobel—looks like it went well," said Zak. "I'm going to do the same with Ryder."

Sy looked at him. "Why?"

"Because I like Isobel and I like Ryder. I know he messed up, and *he* knows he messed up, so we may as well just move on."

"Impressive," said Sy, liking Zak's level-headed approach.

* * *

A few days later, Sy and Zak made their way to the red tent to celebrate the completion of their Level-1 training units and to obtain their color red. Sy joined the other initiates, filled with excitement and a rewarding sense of achievement to have reached this important milestone.

Taurus appeared. He conjured before their eyes the most incredible seven-colored light spectrum, and from the red portion, shining red stars burst into the air. The stars rained down on them and into their eyes. All Sy could see was intense red, and he felt himself lifted off his feet. When he opened his eyes, his entire body was glowing red—and so were Zak's and the other initiates.

Sy and the other tribers outwardly returned to normal, but he felt different, charged.

Taurus beamed proudly. "The color red is now a part of you. Congratulations, and welcome to Level-2. Your next training session will take place in the orange tent."

After the ceremony, Sy and Zak met Ryder, Xanthia, Raf and Isobel at a triber café in Times Square. Sy noticed that Isobel was still struggling to make eye contact with Ryder, but she seemed in good spirits. Zak sat next to her and took her hand. She smiled and moved closer to him.

When the congratulations were done, they ordered fried calamari and cobb salads, and Ryder filled them in on everything: Gabriel, and Sy's plans to find him and how his only clue resided in a stolen dream, and the meeting with the Custodians. Much to their amazement, he told the story of how they'd followed a dream demon all the way to Egypt and come to the conclusion that the *Book of Dreams* was hidden under a pyramid.

"Sounds like the pyramid is in the Valley of the Kings," said Zak. "I went there last summer with my family."

"I thought the pharaohs were buried inside the pyramids," said Isobel, putting some salad on Xanthia's plate and then serving herself.

"They were, initially," Zak said, putting his fork in her salad and picking out some chicken. "But they were moved to tombs to protect them against grave robbers."

"We intend to go back, get inside the Book and find Sy's dream," Ryder said, and he looked at them each in turn, aware that they would think he was nuts.

"Bloody hell!" said Zak.

Raf started firing questions at them. "When are you going? What do you know about Incubus? How will you get in the Book?"

"We're still a bit loose on the details," Ryder admitted, looking at Raf strangely. The hardline attitude was unlike him.

Xanthia looked worried. "You need a watertight plan," she said.

They settled back into their seats and ordered another round of sodas and two large platters of nachos with spicy chili sauce.

"I read somewhere that scorpions have six to twelve eyes, but they don't have good eyesight. They prefer the darkness to harsh light," said Zak, putting his arm around Isobel.

It seemed to Sy that Zak was very eager for everyone to know that he liked Isobel, and Sy was relieved that she seemed quite happy with his display of affection.

"Just watch out for their tails," Zak warned. "Coz that's where they store the venom."

"Enough with the scorpions," said Ryder. "I'm trying to eat."

Things got more serious when they brainstormed possible scenarios should they happen to encounter Incubus.

"But if you get your dream, you can both just get

out of there, right?" asked Xanthia anxiously. "You don't have to face the Dream Sorcerer, do you?"

"I hope not," said Ryder, wiping his hands on his jeans. "Our plan is to get in, get Sy's dream, and get out as quickly as possible. We'll give you updates on the I.N.C."

But they all knew that it wasn't going to be that easy.

16

Inside the Book of Dreams

Thanksgiving came and went, and the holiday season was officially declared. Manhattan transformed into a winter wonderland with Christmas decorations appearing all over the city, and the giant tree was up at the Rockefeller Center.

"Do you want to go skating under the tree?" Sy asked his parents one morning over breakfast.

"I thought you were too cool for that these days," said Trent, sipping his coffee.

"I think we should keep the tradition going," said Sy. They looked surprised. He put his arm around Rebecca. "Mom, are you in?"

He went to brush his teeth, enjoying the pleasure he saw on his parents' faces. It was all about compromise. The balance between his need to be treated as a young adult versus their need to keep him a kid . . . living a life in both realms had matured Sy, he reckoned. He'd experienced crazy situations without his parents—in the Middle Realm he was independent. It was kind of a comfort to have them parent him in the Lower Realm.

Sy was packing his school bag when Ryder appeared on the I.N.C. "Have you seen the news this morning?" he asked.

"No," said Sy.

"Dax and LB have disappeared!"

"What do you mean, disappeared?" asked Sy.

"Like completely vanished," said Ryder. "It's gone viral. No one knows where they are, and there's a major search on. The FBI's involved!"

Everywhere Sy went, newspapers and TV shows were dedicated to speculating on their disappearance, and the Internet had gone nuts on the subject. The police were at a loss—there was no concrete sign of foul play.

In the Middle Realm, it was all anyone could talk about too. They were still missing at the Sagittarius lunar festival a week later.

But for Sy, everything was overshadowed by their plan to get his dream back. Things were getting intense. The gang met several times over the month to pore over the fine details of the plan, trying to make sure that every possible scenario was covered, but they were running out of time.

When the day to put their plan into action finally arrived, Sy couldn't concentrate on anything but the coming evening. He had trouble listening in class and almost got detention several times. He spent lunch break alone, pacing restlessly, going over and over everything in his mind. He'd I.N.C.'d Ryder so many times that Ryder (who was having his own issues concentrating) made him promise not to call again until they met later.

Samuel had organized a restaurant dinner that evening as a way of thanking Rebecca and Trent for having him and Ryder over for meals so often. They met at a Mexican restaurant on Second Avenue at around six-thirty, and by then both Sy and Ryder were freaking out. They kept looking at their phones to check the time and couldn't be led into any conversation. Ryder couldn't make a decision on what to order, which was unheard of.

The adults exchanged puzzled looks. "What is wrong with you tonight?" asked Samuel, exasperated.

"Nothing," Ryder lied.

"Well, what's your order then?" Samuel pointed to the waitress who was waiting, pen poised.

"Tortilla chips and guacamole," said Ryder reluctantly. "I'm really not very hungry."

Samuel gave him a sharp look but said nothing, ordering the fish for himself.

Sy didn't know how he would eat either. He kept smiling at his parents, scared this might be the last time he'd ever see them.

"So, Ryder, have you thought about which colleges you're interested in?" asked Trent.

"Nope," said Ryder, tapping his foot nervously under the table.

"You've still got plenty of time," said Trent kindly.

"Yep, thanks." Ryder answered. "Sy, do you want dessert?"

"Not for me."

"Okay then," said Ryder, getting up abruptly and knocking over his chair with a loud clatter. "Grandpa, can we leave now?"

Samuel, looking furious, paid the check. "Don't forget to wear black," whispered Ryder, and then literally dragged his grandfather to a cab.

It felt like a long trip home, but Sy managed to avoid any serious conversation by asking the cab driver a lot of questions. As soon as they arrived, and before Trent could corner him, Sy pleaded a headache and went to bed. He surprised his parents by embracing them both in a tight bear hug, something he hadn't done in ages.

"I hope you're not coming down with something," said Rebecca, putting her hand on his forehead to check his temperature. And in that moment, her cool hand soothed his nerves.

* * *

A few hours later, he and Ryder met at basecamp.

"Samuel was so pissed at me," said Ryder, pulling

his backpack off and double-checking it had everything they'd need. "I have to call your parents tomorrow to apologize for my behavior."

"That's if we're alive tomorrow," said Sy, his stomach all tied up in knots.

Ryder closed his backpack and held up the picture Zak had given them. Zak was standing with his parents, smiling at the camera in the Valley of the Kings. They were just about to jump in when the *Galaxy Connect Alert* symbol flashed simultaneously on their I.N.C.'s. They each looked at their individual screens to check the announcement.

A temporary freeze has been placed on all accounts due to a virus that has infiltrated the network. You will be unable to send or receive communications or deliveries. The network will be down until further notice. Apologies for any inconvenience.

"I.N.C. not working!" said Sy, in disbelief. "What are we going to do?"

"Maybe we should postpone?" Ryder said, knowing that Sy would never go for it.

"No way," said Sy. "The end of the zodiac year is close, and what if we can't do it this time and have to go back again? We're running out of time."

Xanthia called their names, and they turned around. "Did you get the message about the I.N.C.?" she asked, looking prettier than ever in jeggings, riding boots and a pale blue sweater. Her long blonde hair spilled becomingly around her face. "You have to change your plans," she said.

Ryder felt his chest tighten when he looked at her. "Xanthia, we're still going."

Sy saw that she didn't want to believe it. Her eyes darkened, and then filled with tears.

"We'll be fine," said Ryder, hoping it was true.

"Of course you will," she said, recovering and blinking her tears away. She wrapped her arms around his neck and pulled him close. "Be careful," she whispered.

"We'll be fine," Ryder repeated, forcing himself to concentrate on what lay ahead and not the fact that she was pressing against him.

"Look after yourself, Sy," she said, and hugged him tightly. He was touched by her concern, and he could smell her perfume. He knew exactly why Ryder was hooked.

"We've really gotta go," said Ryder.

Sy looked at the picture of the pyramids, tracing their triangular outline with his fingertips. He held onto Ryder and they jumped inside . . .

They were standing in the heart of the barren valley, the mountains of Thebes in the distance. They flew slowly across the rocky terrain to the pyramid and headed for the entrance they'd used on their last visit.

"Ready?" whispered Ryder, his heart racing. They were arriving a lot earlier than last time, which was part of their plan. Ryder reasoned that a lot of the dream demons wouldn't have finished making their rounds, and he wanted as much of a chance as possible to enter the pyramid undetected.

Sy nodded. He breathed deeply to calm his nerves and thought he knew exactly how the Knicks felt in the playoffs. Every nerve in his body tingled.

They made their way carefully down the inside of the pyramid walls, keeping a sharp eye out for scorpions. They paused at the same indentation in the wall that they'd found last time. The pyramid was dark. As their eyes adjusted, they saw the outline of the scorpions flying along the inner floor of the pyramid, no doubt guarding the Book. They watched in silence, dreading the inevitable confrontation.

"Get ready . . ." whispered Ryder. "*Now!*"

Ryder and Sy held their palms to the center of the pyramid, filling it with the same ultraviolet green light that guided them to basecamp. Ryder had manipulated the light particles to make them lethal, something Samuel had developed in his lab for killing mosquitoes.

"We've got to hit them in the eye," said Ryder, his face screwed in concentration. The light disturbed the scorpions, and they paused for a few tense seconds. "Come on," muttered Ryder, watching them, praying their plan would work.

The scorpions recovered, moving instinctively toward the ledge where Sy and Ryder were standing. If possible, they seemed even more enraged, the bright light infuriating them. Some turned on each other aggressively and attacked, crushing shells with razor-sharp pincers. It seemed like hundreds of them were buzzing furiously, heading straight for them, their stingers ready.

"*Keep shining the light on them*," Ryder instructed, as the buzzing grew louder.

Taking his cue from Ryder, Sy held his palm steady, moving the light beam methodically and shining it directly in their eyes. He felt like things were happening in slow motion and mentally thanked Xanthia for teaching him to be precise and to stay cool in a crisis.

And then it happened! The scorpions closest to them exploded, drenching them in slimy gray goo. "*Don't stop!*" Ryder ordered, wiping his face with his sleeve.

Sy ignored the slime and watched in horrified fascination as scorpions exploded all around them. Finally, there were none left. They were exhausted from the effort and breathed a huge sigh of relief.

"That was *awesome*! We literally blew them up," said Sy, feeling charged.

"Thanks to Zak's detailed knowledge," said Ryder.

He closed his eyes tight, ready to put the next part of their plan into operation. He began by recalling a dream he'd had a few nights ago: a dream he'd had many times and knew in every detail. Asta had told them there was a strong connection between a dream and its dreamer. Ryder asked his dream to come back to him . . .

The floor of the pyramid became transparent. Underneath was the *Book of Dreams*, its pages open as Ryder's dream tried in vain to return to him. "It's working," said Sy excitedly. "I just saw the Book open under the floor."

Ryder continued to concentrate hard on his dream. Beads of sweat broke out on his forehead. Sy saw the Book open again with flashes of color and blurred images. And all the while, the floor remained transparent. "Ryder, your dream is there. Let's go," said Sy urgently, unable to wait a minute longer.

They flew toward the Book, landing on the sandy floor. Ryder was concentrating with all his might on his dream, and by doing so, he kept the floor transparent. Sy grabbed Ryder's arm and they dove inside the Book.

Enormous, the entrance to the Book was dimly lit, but they could see it was built of black granite and marble, with giant spiral pillars, shiny black marble floors and grand, high ceilings—like the foyer of a majestic cathedral.

There was no sign of Ryder's dream.

The Dream Sorcerer's evil magic had completely

infiltrated the Book. All around were blackened statues of ancient Sleep Custodians, and it was dark, cold and ominous. Ryder pulled out the turquoise disk. Blueprint-type grid lines appeared with a miniature holographic image of Asta standing in their center. "You're in the main foyer," she instructed. "Continue straight ahead."

Ryder looked around nervously. "Let's go get your dream," he said.

They flew cautiously, noticing the many arched exits that led to unknown places, grateful for Asta's guidance. As they flew deeper inside the Book, the blueprints changed to reflect where they were. It was quiet and very cold, and they shivered.

"Just before you get to where the dreams are stored, you'll see a giant statue. This is in tribute to the original Custodian who first discovered how to record a dream and created the Book," said Asta.

A few minutes later they flew past the statue, relieved to find it was exactly where she had instructed.

"Take the first exit on your left," she said.

Sy felt excited to be on their way, but as they flew through the arch, they were flung backward, falling with a thud to the granite floor. The turquoise disk slid from Ryder's hand and hit the floor, splitting in two. Asta and the blueprint disappeared. Dream demons closed in on them from every side. One exhaled black fluid from its mouth, straight at Ryder.

"*Forcefield*!" Ryder screamed, but nothing happened.

Sy tackled Ryder and knocked him to the ground. The toxic acid hit a pillar instead, dissolving the granite.

"Damn," whispered Sy as more demons glided in close. "We need to get through that barrier." Frantically, he reached into his pocket and pulled out some dust from the gold silk bag. He threw it at the demons, who froze in their tracks.

"Hurry," said Ryder. "They'll unfreeze any second." He grabbed Sy, threw more dust at the archway and they were able to fly through. Sy looked back to see demons shaking themselves out of their enchantment.

They flew down the hallway, aware there was no more help coming from Asta. The demons were hot in pursuit, and there were so many of them. "Quick, over here," said Ryder, and they hid behind an enormous statue, not daring to breathe . . .

The demons glided past them. They waited a few minutes, but it seemed the coast was clear. Ryder was uneasy. "How come the demons just drifted away?" he asked quietly.

In the walls of the corridor, hundreds of archways led to other corridors, sorted by name in alphabetical order, as well as date and time. It was systematic and orderly, like a library reference system.

They flew around for a while, searching for Sy's

name. When they found it, they found the most recent dreams were first. It was overwhelming to see how many of his dreams had been recorded in his short life. They looked left and right, searching for the correct month and day.

"This is it," said Sy, stopping at a small black door. "This is exactly when I had my dream."

He was thrilled that they'd managed to find it, but Ryder was on edge. It all seemed too easy! He tried to open the door, but it was locked.

"What do we do now?" asked Sy, feeling panicked.

Ryder tried some magic dust, with no luck.

"This can't be happening—we're so close," said Sy desperately.

"You do it," said Ryder. "You're the rightful owner, so you should be able to open the door."

Sy touched the handle cautiously. It was immediate; they could hear things happening inside the lock. He looked at Ryder expectantly.

"Go for it," he whispered. "Just hurry!"

Sy's heart was pounding. He'd never seen Ryder so freaked out. "I'll be quick, I promise," he said. He pushed open the door. Despite his best effort, it closed behind him and the last thing he saw was Ryder on guard, his eyes darting around, left to wait impatiently.

* * *

Inside the room, it was quiet and strangely serene. Sy didn't know what he'd been expecting but it certainly wasn't this. Fragments of his dream were floating around the room like giant jigsaw pieces. On each piece, images were moving in slow motion, like an old home video. He stood mesmerized, trying to work out what to do. Then it hit him. It really was a puzzle and he needed to solve it. But how could he, when he couldn't remember the dream?

But Ryder was out there guarding him with his life. Taking a deep breath, Sy looked at the pieces floating in front of him with a fresh eye, trying to see which was first and willing himself to remember. He captured an image, and as soon as he touched it, the piece froze on the spot. He looked around thoughtfully at the other fragments, trying to recall any detail, but his mind remained blank; he found it wandering to things like what time it was and how long he'd been in the room. He shook his head to clear it and focused his energy on the puzzle. Slowly, he began putting pieces together.

It was time-consuming work until he realized that when he was correct, the piece would lock in place, but if he were wrong, it would just continue to float around the room. He stopped trying to figure out the overall image and worked fast, focusing on color and shape. Bit by bit, the dream began to come together.

Sparkling turquoise water, giant waves . . . and

then a small island, the tar-like substance and a figure that was desperate to give him something despite his dire predicament; holding up a golden flower-like device, engraved with an intricate design.

It dawned on Sy . . . this was the vision he'd seen the night he had learned about Gabriel! Had he dreamed it again the night it was stolen? He hadn't even considered that possibility, even though the vision had plagued him since he'd first seen it. With mounting excitement, Sy knew he was about to come face to face with his brother.

That first time, he hadn't realized there was more to the picture—and then he'd found himself in Dreamtime and Taurus had been there—but here it was again, floating all around him. He couldn't make out the face; it must be still hidden in the diminishing number of pieces. He worked quickly, and finally put the last piece in place; the image of his brother was complete. He drew back in disbelief.

The face staring back at him was his own.

How was that possible? Was *he* Gabriel? The dream-boy held the golden flower in his palm; it was octagon in shape and on it were eight points. Sy thought it looked like some type of compass. The figure spoke:

The rose-shaped compass is the key,
It will destroy the evil and set you free.
Use the dust to find the Seal,

Be wary of what is illusion and what is real.
The four-point compass is ancient,
Its power is vast,
Move the points anti-clockwise,
Save the north point for last.

The figure screamed as it was swallowed up by the black tar. Sy's dream shook and then shattered. The tiny pieces struck him and were absorbed by his body. His dream was inside him. He was able to easily recall every image, every word.

He didn't have time to address the sickening disappointment that, after everything they had done to find his brother, Gabriel must have died in the encroaching sludge. Or had he just seen a vision of himself? If so, why was he told he'd dreamed of his brother?

He took a deep breath and pushed open the door, eager to share his dream and its riddle with Ryder, but the corridor was empty.

Ryder had vanished.

17

Betrayal

"Ryder!" called Sy urgently, his panic mounting, no longer caring if he was heard. His palm flashed with the sixty-minute warning . . . only an hour before Dreamtime was over. What if Ryder was captured? He had to find him. He raced up the corridor looking left and right, but there was no sign of him and everything looked the same.

He stopped and regained his breath, forcing his mind to think clearly. He tried to I.N.C. the others, but it was still down. Where could Ryder be? Perhaps if he headed to the Heart of the Book he'd have a chance of finding the Great Seal, which might then help him find Ryder. If he didn't find him soon, they'd both be trapped in the Book forever. But without Asta, how was he going to find the Heart of the Book?

Sy drifted around in a daze of fear. Desperate, he flew through several chambers with no clear sense of where he was going, sure he was running out of time.

He wanted to get into the Heart of the Book but ended up back in the foyer where he and Ryder had first entered. He felt a sharp pain in his gut at how much their friendship had come to mean to him. Ryder had gone out on a limb for him by coming here. Sy really didn't know where to go next. He froze, his confidence shattered, overcome by guilt that his stubborn insistence had forced Ryder into helping him.

He felt a hand on his shoulder and looked up, startled, hoping against hope that it was Ryder, and was stunned to find Raf standing over him, smiling. "Raf!" he exclaimed in relief. "What are you doing here?" He was thrilled to see him and overwhelmed with gratitude. Raf always seemed to be there for him when he really needed it most.

"I thought you might need some help," Raf said. "The others were worried, given the I.N.C. is down."

Sy exhaled in relief. Raf would get them out of this mess. "I'm so glad you're here. Ryder's missing. I think Incubus has got him, and there isn't much time left to find him before we're all lost in the Book forever," he blurted. "We need to find the Heart of the Book."

"Okay, let's get going then," said Raf. "How about we try up there?" He gestured to a corridor guarded by Sleep Custodian statues in striking warrior poses that Sy hadn't seen before. Sy felt a great surge of hope now that he had some support.

But it didn't take long for his elation to fade.

"Raf, are you sure we aren't lost?" he asked as they flew down yet another endless corridor.

"Trust me, I have a hunch we're close," said Raf. Moments later, he stopped at a small black door. "After you," he said, smiling.

Sy hesitated. All of a sudden, he felt uneasy. He couldn't work out why, except that Raf's smile did not make it to his eyes.

"Just in here," Raf encouraged.

What was happening? Sy's intuition was warning him, but his brain was stubbornly resisting. This was reliable Raf, with his same sandy hair and freckles. Why should he be feeling so threatened all of a sudden? Sy opened the door slightly and paused, stalling, his mind ticking over. He peered into the room. It was dark, but then he made out movement, as if the darkened room had a glimmering, silver floor.

He glanced back at Raf, remembering that during his martial arts training he was taught to listen to his inner voice and trust his instincts. "So, Raf," he said, trying to keep his voice light, "how did you get into the Book?"

Raf looked taken aback at Sy's question. "I followed a dream demon like you and Ryder did," he said.

"You're lying," accused Sy. "There's no way you could have got into the Book unless someone told you how."

Raf didn't answer. In a rush of clarity, Sy knew his hunch was right. Raf had insider knowledge of dream demons, or maybe even of Incubus! His mind reeled at the enormity of what that might mean. He looked back into the room. The glimmers of light were coming closer, as if sensing the potential release of the partially opened door. Sy turned back to Raf. They stood, tense, staring at each another.

Raf lunged and hit him, smack on the jaw. Sy felt like he'd been knocked with a jackhammer. He fell against the door, closing it. "Are you crazy?"

Raf didn't answer, just stared at Sy threateningly, his eyes narrowed. Jumping to his feet, Sy held his hands up defensively, praying his new karate black belt would prove useful. He blocked Raf's left-hook punch and spun around, elbowing Raf in the face. Raf didn't even flinch. Instead, he retaliated with swift, precise movements, striking Sy in the chest and head.

Sy staggered blindly and Raf opened the door. Sy heard a low buzz that froze his insides as Raf smiled sadistically and moved in for the kill. Summoning the small amount of strength he had left, Sy flew up and out of the way. Raf lost his footing and crashed head-first through the black doorway.

Sy covered his ears against the sound of Raf's screams as hundreds of enraged giant scorpions attacked. The screams stopped and the scorpions turned to the door, coming for Sy. There was nothing he could do but slam it shut. He turned away, sickened, and started running blindly.

What if Raf had . . . what if Ryder had been attacked by the scorpions? He couldn't bear the thought. He had to believe Ryder was still alive. A black shaft opened up at Sy's feet and he fell, closing his eyes, sure now that this was the end.

He landed with a painful thud on a marble floor. He looked around, panicked, but there was no one, no clacking scorpions buzzing in the dark. He sat there, regaining his breath, and saw he was facing a small door made of solid gold.

Sy's pulse quickened. He fumbled in his jeans pocket for the magic dust, his brother's words imprinted in his mind:

> The rose-shaped compass is the key,
> It will destroy the evil and set you free.
> Use the dust to find the seal,
> Be wary of what is illusion and what is real.
> The four-point compass is ancient,
> Its power is vast,
> Move the points anti-clockwise,
> Save the north point for last.

He'd never been so petrified in his life, but time was running out. He recited the Custodian command and waited. The door swung open. This section of the Book had a completely different look and feel. It was all white, with a sense of serenity and positive energy.

Asta had been right; it was obviously how the Book used to be when the Custodians had controlled it. The stark contrast between this space and the rest of the Book made him feel safer. He allowed himself a small frisson of hope.

Bathed in white light, Sy slowly paced out eighteen steps, as he had been instructed, careful not to make them too big or too small. He looked at the floor where he should find the hidden compass, the Golden Seal. Praying it was the correct spot, he threw some of the dust.

The white floor dissolved, revealing a large, ornate golden rose: a compass with thirty-two points. Ancient symbols and numbers indicated the four main points of the compass. Two ancient Custodian warrior statues on each side came to life, pulled steel swords from scabbards on their backs and flew off, reciting what sounded like a war chant.

"Hold up!" called Sy. "Come back and tell me what to do!" He waited a few seconds, but all was quiet; he was on his own.

Taking a deep breath, he recalled his brother's instructions and moved the four compass points in a three-hundred-and-sixty degree anti-clockwise direction, re-locking them back in place, careful to end with the north point. He positioned his palm directly in the center of the rose. The instant he connected with the compass, all thirty-two points began to spin and separate from the circular base, rising up.

He heard a soft moaning. Sy could hardly believe his eyes: there, on the floor at the base of the compass, was Ryder! He was breathing evenly and looked unharmed, just asleep. Sy stood staring, shocked but relieved to see him safe.

"Ryder," he called, reaching in to shake him roughly, but nothing happened. "*Ryder*," he shouted more urgently. "Wake up!"

But it was no use. Nothing he did could rouse him.

18

Incubus

Sy shook Ryder again, willing him to wake up. Maybe the Golden Seal would help. He pulled it from the compass and held it up for a closer look. Beams of light intersected, crossing and connecting the eight outer edges. As he held the Seal in his hand, it shrank and felt weightless. Sy turned joyously to Ryder, hoping that the Seal's magic could awaken him.

A dark shadow loomed over his shoulder, blocking the light. With a sick feeling, Sy shoved the Seal in his pocket. Reluctantly, he turned. The Dream Sorcerer towered over him. At least nine feet tall, he wore black hooded robes, and where his eyes and hands should have been was only shimmering, silver fluid.

Sy stared transfixed. The silver shimmer became clearer and clearer, and Sy felt himself sinking into blackness. The Dream Sorcerer faded into the background, replaced by another image: a silhouette that took his breath away.

Gabriel held his hands out to Sy and spoke his name. It still felt strange to be face to face with his brother, but Sy's heart danced with happiness. Sy took a step toward him and clasped his brother's hands, never wanting to let go.

"We'll be together soon," Gabriel said. "And you'll know the truth about me."

Sy's voice was no more than a whisper. "Are you alive?"

"I'm closer than you may think," Gabriel replied.

Sy wished with all his heart that this moment would not end and he could stay like this forever, reunited with the sibling he'd been longing for.

"You're dreaming," his brother told him. "Incubus is using me to trap you. You must break the connection with me so you can wake up."

"No," Sy refused. "I've finally found you, and I'm not losing you again."

"Sy, wake up," Gabriel insisted. "You'll see me again, I promise."

"*No*," said Sy stubbornly, willing himself to remain in this blissful dream-state where nothing mattered and everything was perfect.

"Sy —"

"No!"

"Break the connection—you have to trust me." Gabriel's voice was penetrating and loud, and hurt his head, ruining his peace. "Wake up . . . *save Ryder.*"

Ryder.

Gabriel was right: he had no choice. He took a deep breath and, even though it broke his heart, let go of his brother's hand.

Jarred back to the present, he found himself lying on the floor with Incubus looming over him. Sy avoided the sorcerer's eyes and rolled away. He jumped to his feet, keeping his face averted, and took off. To his horror, he was pulled back to Incubus like a magnet and was forced to stare into the Dream Sorcerer's shimmering, liquid eyes, his own eyes widening in terror.

Something roughly grabbed the back of his shirt and tossed him, spinning in midair. He lost all sense of up and down. When it stopped, he gagged; he was in an elevator and it was going up. His chest tight, his heart pounding, he broke into a sweat. He was alone in a cramped space and his claustrophobia was suffocating. This was worse than any other time. Stifled, he knew he was going to choke and die. He started wheezing as his breath came in short sharp bursts. His head was going to explode, and his legs gave way, forcing him to his knees in the corner of the elevator. It raced upward.

In the midst of his panic, Gabriel's calm voice came unbidden into his mind and penetrated his fear. *Conquer your fear to seal his fate . . . save Ryder . . .*

Understanding blossomed: saving Ryder was paramount.

Sy knew what he had to do. "I have no fear. This is an illusion!" he shouted, over and over with a ferocious intensity until his voice was hoarse. At last, the emergency stop button came into his focus, and he pushed it with all his might. The elevator lurched to a stop with a massive jolt.

Sy stood, listening, his breathing returning to normal. He pushed the button to open the doors, and they slid back to reveal a black emptiness. He closed his eyes, took a leap of faith and jumped into the darkness . . .

Again, he found himself face to face with Incubus. The Dream Sorcerer's visage was filled with a terrifying fury, but this time Sy was unafraid. If he could survive that elevator, he could survive anything! Reaching into his pocket, he pulled out the Golden Seal. Incubus raised his arm to strike and, instinctively, Sy held up the Seal like a ward against the evil.

Sy recoiled in horror, his mouth forced open against his will, his chest pulsating. It felt like something was being extracted from deep inside him. He coughed and retched until a mini-twister was expelled from his mouth in a great gush. It was threaded with fire, and wrapped inside it was water mixed with dirt. Sy, panting with exertion, stared amazed as the four elements of air, earth, fire and water sped toward his enemy.

Incubus was caught up in the twister and choked

by the water; fire crept up his robes, and earth blinded his shimmering eyes.

While the sorcerer screamed in agony and fury, Sy threw the Golden Seal directly at him. It spun gracefully through the air and, with each rotation, increased to its original size. Each of its points pierced the silver fluid, sending it splashing over the white floor. Incubus, with a last blood-curdling cry, exploded into hundreds of pieces, which were sucked into the heart of the Seal. Thousands of dream demons followed him, flowing like vapors, disappearing into the Seal; chased into it by the Seal's guards, wielding their swords.

Quiet now, the Golden Seal shrank and returned like a boomerang to Sy's outstretched hand. Sy grasped it carefully and returned it to its rightful place.

He knelt by Ryder, who now lay on the floor at his feet. All around them, walls were crumbling. Sy guessed the Book was returning to its original state now that the evil had been vanquished. But he didn't care about the *Book of Dreams*, only about his friend. He hardly dared touch him, terrified that he was dead.

"Ryder?" he managed, his voice thick with tears.

Ryder opened his turquoise eyes and a familiar cheeky grin transformed his handsome face. "That was some dream I was having," he said. "What did I miss?"

19

The Truth

As far as Sy and Ryder were concerned, the following night seemed too soon to receive a formal command to meet with their Zodiac Council representatives. The boys were emotionally and physically exhausted, and nervous about the meeting, but sort of relieved, too. They were both still in deep shock about Raf, and struggling to come to terms with his betrayal and gruesome demise. Ryder's pained face revealed how deeply he felt the loss of someone he'd considered a close and trusted friend.

Sy, too, was taking it hard. It was difficult to imagine trusting anyone again. He'd never had a lot of friends, and he treasured each one. He kept reliving Raf's last moments and could not get the scorpions and their attack out of his mind.

They waited, as requested, outside Taurus's personal tent.

"I hope we're not in any trouble," said Ryder.

"Me, too." Sy yawned. "You don't think they'll expel us, do you?"

"Enter," called Virgo.

"Well," said Ryder. "We're about to find out."

Inside they were met with smiles—and Samuel talking to their Earth-tribe leaders! Samuel grinned at them, and Sy immediately felt at ease.

Ryder's shoulders relaxed. Samuel's presence was like a tonic. Even if they were in trouble, his grandpa would have their backs.

Virgo gestured to them to sit down. "You have been through a harrowing experience," she said. "Your selflessness allowed you to succeed. The power of friendship, love and loyalty you showed each other enabled you to face evil and emerge victorious."

Taurus tossed his mighty head. "Throughout your ordeal, you conducted yourselves with the integrity we expect of a triber. You have brought great honor to the Earth-tribe," he said.

Sy smiled in relief at this unexpected praise. Samuel beamed at him and at Ryder.

"Sy, you have conquered an extraordinary fear," Taurus went on. "You have learned that you can be confident in your own ability to make the right choices. You should feel proud of these achievements."

"I had help," Sy admitted. When he thought of Gabriel, his throat constricted with emotion.

Capricorn nodded, his eyes sparkling. "Asta tells

us the *Book of Dreams* has been safely returned to the Custodians and is restored to full working order. A significant benefit to all living creatures," he said.

"What about Raf?" said Sy.

There was a pause.

"The person who attacked you in the *Book of Dreams* was not your friend Raf, but his clone," said Taurus. "You saw the laboratory. The Darkforce found a way to clone Raf . . ."

Sy was stunned and horrified that Raf had been cloned, and wondered what that meant for the real Raf; but he was relieved, too, to think it wasn't his friend who had suffered that grisly death.

Ryder's face was deathly pale. When could this have happened? How had none of them realized? "Where's the real Raf?" he asked quietly.

"We are searching for him and believe he is still alive," said Taurus, his tone still gentle.

Sy felt himself choke up. It was his fault. The Darkforce abducted Raf to try and get to him . . .

"Sy, you are not responsible," said Taurus, reading his anguished thoughts. "The cloned Raf was communicating directly with Incubus, and he's the one who tampered with the I.N.C. The Dream Sorcerer was expecting you."

Ryder cringed at the violation of Raf being taken by the Darkforce. And what kind of friend was he that he hadn't noticed any difference when the clone took over?

"The Darkforce has been converting dreams into nightmares and distilling from them some kind of evil substance in order to enhance the pool of negativity they are creating," said Taurus. "And, as you know, they are also using this liquid to create their clones. To fully complete this process and take on a person's identity, they must steal their soul. They have been unable to do this, and rescuing the *Book of Dreams* further thwarts their progress."

Virgo smiled solemnly at Sy. "Your brother was trying to warn you about the pool of negativity and its link to Incubus. He was trying to show you the force of its evil power and how it can hurt humanity. Now that you have defeated Incubus, the pool of negativity is weakened but not completely destroyed."

"The Middle and Lower Realms are still in great danger, and so are you," Capricorn added.

"But where's Gabriel?" Sy blurted. "Is he alive? Why haven't my parents and I been allowed to know him?"

Taurus, Virgo and Capricorn shared a moment of telepathic communion, and Samuel nodded his support.

Taurus spoke softly. "Thirteen years ago, your mother gave birth to two boys. Do you remember I told you that you and your brother are linked to an important event that will affect the future of both realms?"

"Yes."

"The Darkforce also became aware of this prediction and sought to prevent it at all costs. They planned to end your lives during your mother's labor—as complications during the birth."

Sy listened with a mixture of disbelief, anger and sadness. Had his brother been murdered?

Virgo took over, her voice soft and compassionate. "When we learned of their plan, we sent Taurus straight to the hospital," she said. "He was too late to save your brother, but was able to ensure your safe arrival a few minutes later."

"Twins!" he breathed, finally understanding.

"Yes," smiled Virgo.

"My parents?" asked Sy.

"This was a very traumatic time for them. The Council decided to intervene, because this event had occurred unnaturally at the hand of evil. We erased the memories of your parents and all those who knew your mother was expecting twins. Your mom and dad were thrilled to welcome their new baby boy into the world and have loved you dearly ever since."

Sy felt a weird sense of relief. "Where is he now? Can I meet him?" he asked.

"Like you, your brother is impatient for your first meeting," said Taurus. "However, he has agreed to be guided by the Council on this matter."

"The timing is almost right," said Virgo.

"He resides in spirit form. That's how he found a way to communicate with you via your dreams," added Taurus.

Sy wanted to protest, but then he thought of the message his brother had given him in the elevator. It was his guidance that had helped Sy understand that if he could master his claustrophobia, he would be strong enough to defeat Incubus and save Ryder.

"Sy, when you were first initiated as a triber, you received a message from the Nefiot Gnomes," Taurus said. "You were told you had natural gifts. Telepathy is one of them. We teach it to tribers at Level-5, and not all of them are able to master the skill. You and your brother are closely connected, enabling him to penetrate your mind and awaken you inside your dream-state, and possibly enhancing your inherent telepathic abilities."

"I'd like to thank him," said Sy, hopefully.

"You will," Taurus assured him.

"There will be a formal Custodian ceremony in your honor," said Capricorn. "But now, please tell us all about your adventure in the *Book of Dreams* . . ."

* * *

Their friends were waiting for them at a table in the back of the Lounge. They also wanted the story from the beginning, and between them, Sy and Ryder filled them in on all that had happened.

Raf's absence was palpable. The shock of what had happened to him overshadowed everything. Sy's throat ached when he looked at the empty seat at the table. No matter what Taurus said, he was responsible.

"Bloody hell!" said Zak, shaking his head in disbelief, his arm comfortingly around Isobel. Shock and grief had rendered her speechless.

"When could it have happened?" Xanthia asked.

No one knew the answer. Sy could feel the others shared his confusion and guilt that they hadn't noticed. Ryder looked shattered. He was still pale, and his voice was unsteady. Xanthia held his hand.

Sy and Ryder's palms started flashing. "Taurus says there'll be a celebration in a few days, hosted by the Custodians," Sy told them. "And you're all invited."

He really didn't feel like celebrating, knowing that Raf was out there alone, possibly dead, and from the looks on his friends' faces, neither did they. "We can't not go," he said. "Asta would be really offended."

"Thanks, everyone. We couldn't have done it without you," said Ryder.

Sy and Ryder said their goodbyes, feeling more like brothers than ever.

20

Celebration

A few days later it was time for the celebration of the return of the *Book of Dreams*. Asta herself came to escort them to the Custodian palace.

"Bloody brilliant!" said Zak, looking around at the magnificent crystal and gold of the domed palace as the team and Isobel were seated, and Ryder and Sy led off to a VIP box.

The Custodians enacted an ancient ritual in their honor. Hundreds of elite Custodian warriors gave them a hero's salute; their spears were raised, and laser beams shot into the air to form an image of the Golden Seal. This was followed by a stunning fireworks display. The boys saw the silhouettes of Taurus, Virgo and Capricorn beaming down at them.

After the parade, they joined up with the rest of the gang for the sumptuous feast. Some time later, even Ryder couldn't eat another thing. He spotted Xanthia with Asta and walked purposefully toward them. It was time.

Asta smiled at him. "Well, Ryder, how does it feel to have achieved your goal?"

"Well, I haven't. Not quite," he said, and offered Xanthia his hand. "Join me?"

Xanthia took it, and with Asta's smile of approval, Ryder led her away from the crowd to sit in a quiet area of the palace.

"So, you never did tell me what you were dreaming about in the Book," she teased.

"I could tell you about my dream . . ." Ryder moved close and looked at her intently.

Xanthia stared back at him, her blue eyes expectant.

He pulled her close. "But I'd rather show you . . ."

He ran his hands up her arms and held her face gently. She closed her eyes and they kissed. He felt her melt into him and twine her fingers in his hair, as the kiss deepened. Finally, they drew apart and stared into each other's eyes.

"Some dream," she said shakily.

"Xanthia —" Ryder's face was earnest. "You and me . . . I'm not playing you. We were meant to be together." He kissed her again. "Okay?" he said with a firm certainty.

"Okay," she whispered.

They sat together for a long while, fingers entwined, talking about everything and nothing.

"We better get back to the others," said Xanthia finally.

"All right," Ryder agreed reluctantly.

"Can we just keep this to ourselves for a while?" she asked. "It would be nice to figure this out on our own, without judgment. Don't you think?"

He studied her quietly for a few moments, his expression unreadable. "You got it," he said, taking her hand.

They made their way back, the noise of the party getting louder as they came closer.

As they neared the others, Ryder pulled Xanthia into the shadows and kissed her again, long and deep. Then he let go of her hand and, without a backward glance, disappeared into the crowd, leaving a trembling Xanthia staring after him longingly . . .

* * *

The lead-up to Christmas in the Lower Realm carried life along with it. Sy was enjoying exploring his new Level-2 powers, but he missed Raf horribly. Dax and LB were also still missing, and despite all the speculation and rumors, including that they'd formed an alliance with the Darkforce, no one knew what the real story was.

Xanthia's family was in town from Toronto for the weekend, and Ryder was playing tour guide. Sy had arranged to meet the two of them at the New York Public Library. He was at Forty-Second Street when he stopped cold in his tracks.

Ryder and Xanthia were by the great lion statues at the library's entrance in what looked like a heated argument with Dax and LB! After all the press and speculation on their disappearance, it was surreal to see them in the middle of Fifth Avenue in broad daylight. What was going on?

A ball of fire, large as a basketball, came hurtling through the air at his friends. "Move!" bellowed Ryder, pushing Xanthia out of the way and hiding them both behind Fortitude. The fireball narrowly missed the lion statue and smashed on the library steps.

Sy was rooted to the spot in horror. They weren't supposed to be using their powers in the Lower Realm!

"You won't be tribers for much longer," Xanthia shouted at them.

"We're already way ahead of you and the Council," said Dax with an arrogant smirk.

"You and your useless circus freaks should watch your backs. Prepare for war!" said LB furiously.

"Bring it on!" roared Ryder, looking manic.

Scorching flames flew from LB's mouth.

"Forcefield!" screamed Ryder, holding up his palm. The invisible shimmering wall appeared, shielding them.

Sy raced toward them, almost colliding with a cab, the driver cursing loudly. When Sy looked up, the fire had almost penetrated their forcefield! Ryder and Xanthia looked at each other, and Sy could see their panic. Without thinking, he ran at Dax and LB from behind and, with a mighty kick, hit LB in the back. It stopped the fire. When Dax turned to attack, Sy hit him in the stomach, winding him.

Ryder and Xanthia took off, and Dax and LB followed in hot pursuit. "You're done," LB yelled at Sy.

Sy chased them, running furiously, but Ryder was fast and he lost them. He was seriously freaked out. Dax and LB were Level-7 with superior powers, and their capabilities far exceeded that of his friends. As they approached Union Square Park, Dax and LB took flight.

Sy could not believe their audacity. They joined palms midair, creating a powerful fusion of energy. When they moved apart, a volcanic rock had formed, with red-hot molten lava flowing inside it. Flames were leaping off the rock, and it grew in dimension with each second that passed.

Dax threw the blazing projectile. It hit the sidewalk and exploded. Smoke and the sound of screaming shattered the peace as people scattered, terrorized by flames. Sy, recoiling in horror, saw bedlam break out around him.

Dax and LB continued to create fireballs, and the city of Manhattan descended into a state of emergency. Sirens filled the air as the FDNY sped to the scene. Crowds were fleeing and nearby police tried valiantly to clear the area.

Sy caught sight of Ryder and Xanthia in Union Square Park. They were coughing from the smoke and panting with exhaustion. Dax and LB, taking advantage of their confusion, flew toward them and joined palms again. With a smug look of victory, the rebel tribers aimed another fiery rock at them.

Sy was too far away to help. He shouted a warning, and Ryder and Xanthia instinctively created a forcefield. In a panic, Sy I.N.C.'d Samuel and blurted the situation to him. Samuel broke the connection just as the forcefield faltered and failed, unable to resist the power and force of the comet-sized rocks.

A rock exploded, hurling Xanthia and Ryder through the air. Sy's heart leapt in his mouth, Dax and LB grinned at each other in satisfaction and disappeared.

At that same moment, Samuel materialized in the sky, his usually smiling face filled with fury, just in time to catch Ryder and Xanthia, saving them from smashing into a burning building. When he had carried them to safety, Samuel turned his attention to the fires. Within minutes, the raging flames were under control and countless lives saved.

* * *

Back at the Ryderson warehouse, Samuel fussed over Xanthia and Ryder, checking for wounds and making them sip warm, sweet tea. Each had sustained burns, but felt lucky they hadn't been more seriously harmed. Samuel waved his hands over their burns and healed them completely. "Good thinking," he said to Sy. "Thank you for calling me."

Sy's heart swelled. He felt like he'd done one small thing to repay everything Ryder and Xanthia had given him since he'd become a triber. He busied himself with pouring drinks. "What will happen to Dax and LB?" he asked.

"The Council will wipe the memory of anyone who saw them use their powers," said Samuel, his mouth pressed into a firm line. "And then I expect they'll be expelled."

* * *

The Lounge was abuzz with news about what had happened at the New York State Library. Ryder, Xanthia and Sy had been before the Council again to tell them everything, and a delegation from Fire-tribe had been to see both Ryder and Xanthia and their teams to formally apologize and distance themselves from Dax and LB. The Fire-tribers told them that the rebel tribers had been issued with a formal summons by their leader, Leo; they had until the Pisces new moon to appear before the Council.

Xanthia led Sy and the rest of the team out to their training area. "There's nothing we can do about Dax and LB now," she said. "Lunar Pisces is coming and we're one down." Xanthia looked at the team soberly. "We've got a lot of training to do—Zak and Sy are ready to use Level-2 and . . ." Her voice broke. "Let's give this our all . . . for Raf." They huddled in a circle, arms around each other.

"To Raf! To Raf! To Raf!" they chanted.

* * *

Sy was grateful to be home, and to finally understand the truth about Gabriel. Despite his sadness over Raf, he was so glad to be alive that it felt like it was going to be the best Christmas ever.

Samuel and Ryder had become part of their family, and Samuel was spending a lot of time with Sy, helping him come to terms with his trauma over the recent events. "The best way to help yourself is by providing service to others," he said. "I support a number of charities that assist disadvantaged families and orphaned children. Ryder and I help out at some of the local community programs each month."

"I didn't know that," said Sy.

"Some of the children are quite taken with him. He's a real inspiration," Samuel said proudly. "I see how much Ryder benefits from his involvement. You're welcome to join us any time."

"I'd like that," said Sy.

Rebecca cooked a traditional dinner on Christmas Eve, and they exchanged gifts under a fragrant tree adorned with beautiful lights. Levi perched on top of the tree, sharing his opinion on each gift—much to the great amusement of Sy and Ryder. After one wise-crack too many, Samuel frowned at him and he bid them a hasty goodbye.

Sy was thrilled to unwrap a brand new computer. "Awesome!"

"It's your notebook, but it's to be used with our supervision," Trent warned.

"Sure," Sy agreed. "Thanks, Mom and Dad."

When the presents were done, they toasted the contracts being signed on Trent and Samuel's new film.

When Sy and Ryder took his new computer into Sy's room, he got the fright of his life. Gabriel was sitting on his bed. It was like looking in the mirror, except that Gabriel's skin was very pale: *ghostlike*, Sy thought, and he seemed fragile.

Sy couldn't take his eyes off him. His throat tightened and he felt overcome with emotion.

"You must be Gabriel," said Ryder, moving toward the bed and holding out his hand. "I'm Ryder."

Gabriel stood up and held out his hand to shake, but his eyes were glued on Sy.

"Brother," he said quietly.

Sy ran toward him and threw his arms around him. He felt cold and too thin, but Sy didn't care. Gabriel was in his room!

"I'm not meant to be here, and I can't stay long," said Gabriel. He clasped Sy's hand. "But I just had to come. It's Christmas after all." He smiled sadly.

"Did you see Mom and Dad?" Sy asked carefully, well aware of the cruel truth that he was part of the Middleton family and Gabriel was not.

"Only briefly. Your grandpa doesn't miss a trick," he told Ryder.

Ryder nodded. "Tell me about it."

Gabriel turned to Sy, looking serious. "I can't come again until Taurus gives us formal permission." He held up his hand to block Sy's protest. "I won't put you in danger."

"But Incubus is dead."

"It's just a set-back for the Darkforce," said Gabriel. "We're not in the clear yet."

"Are you all right?" Sy wanted to know. "Are you safe?"

"Yes. Look after him," Gabriel told Ryder, clearly reluctant to leave as his thin body became even more transparent.

"Don't go —" said Sy, but Gabriel vanished right before his eyes.

Sy went to the window and looked out into the cold night. "I'm going to find a way to reunite my family," he said with a steely determination in his voice that Ryder had never heard before. "And you know who else we're going to find?"

Ryder nodded, breaking into one of his careless grins. "Raf," he said.

* * *

Sy and Ryder spent New Year's Eve in Times Square among millions of other New Yorkers and tourists who braved the freezing conditions to celebrate another new beginning. Sy was constantly hoping that Gabriel would appear, but he had not seen or heard from him. Thousands of magical creatures partied throughout the city alongside the unsuspecting humans. They'd created their own clubs and lounges, and the giant amusement park that sat over the city was packed to capacity. Goblins were dancing on top of the New Year's Eve Ball and around the flagpole.

Before the countdown, Levi appeared and insisted they join his private rave at a venue floating above the Plaza Hotel.

"Great, we'll see you there later," said Ryder.

"And bring Xanthia!" shouted Levi, drowned out as fireworks lit up the Manhattan skyline and the crowd roared with wonder and appreciation.

Sy felt like the luckiest kid in the world.